RING OF WARRIORS

~MAKING A FIGHTER~

Marcus Blake

BOOK 1

Ring of Warriors: Making a Fighter

A Mavericknes Media / Truesource Publishing book

Ring of Warriors: Making a Fighter
Carol Felder and J M Almgreen

The story is fictional and any resemblance to actual people,
places, and certain facts associated with the characters
created by Marcus Blake is purely coincidence.

Mavericknes Media : Dallas Texas

 Truesource Publishing : Dallas Texas

www.truesourcepublishing.com

ISBN : 978-1-932996-53-1

Printed in the United States of America
Published in Dallas, Texas

For More information on Marcus Blake go to….

www.marcusblake.net
www.facebook.com/themarcusblake
www.twitter.com/marcusblake
www.thatnerdshow.com

About the Author

Marcus Blake was born in Chicago, Illinois in 1977. He grew up in Chicago and East Texas. His education is in History, Literature, Psychology, and Religion & Philosophy. Marcus Blake has studied at many universities throughout the United States, but his Alma Mater is Stephen F. Austin State University in Nacogdoches, Texas, which is also where he wrote his first book, The Music of Life. Marcus Blake is a Poet, Musician, Comedian, Writer, and Historian. His books are The Music of Life, My Reflections, Returning Home. Sex Game. The Lonely Girl, Stories From Wrigley, 30 Minutes: Trust and Lies, 30 Minutes: Guilty Until Proven Innocent, 30 Minutes: A Soldier's Song, and 30 Minutes: A Badge of Honor. . He has taught in the public school system, served in the Army, and been a guest speaker at Education and Literary events throughout the world. Marcus Blake is also a Radio Host, his current show is Saturday Morning Nerd Show which can be heard on Saturday Mornings at www.thatnerdshow.com. He is a veteran of Rock and Roll shows as well as Political shows on the radio. Marcus Blake makes his home in the Dallas, Texas .

Other Books by Marcus Blake...

The Music of Life

My Reflections

Returning Home

Sex Game

The Lonely Girl

Stories From Wrigley

30 Minutes: Trust and Lies

30 Minutes: Guilty Until Proven Innocent

30 Minutes: A Soldier's Song

30 Minutes: A Badge of Honor

This book is dedicated to the fighters who
have the courage to step inside the ring,
take a beating, and keep coming back.

The true definition of a warrior!

PROLOGUE

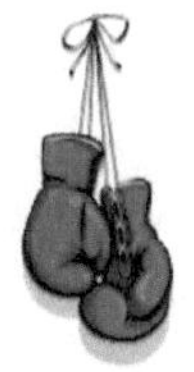

Fighters have to Fight! That's the most important lesson I ever learned about boxing from my grandfather. Sure, there's strategy, calculation, and superb conditioning when it comes to boxing, but for the two guys inside of the ring it boils down to one simple truth... fighters have to fight. And the courage that it takes to get inside that ring, to take a beating, and to keep going forward, well, there isn't any better metaphor for life. That was another thing he used to tell me. He was big on metaphors when teaching me about life.

I never cared much about boxing growing up. I had to be around it before I was hooked. I had to see it before realizing the true definition of a warrior... at least in terms of sports. A warrior in boxing is someone that rises and falls, only to keep getting back up despite the beatings they endure. That was never more exemplified than with Liam "The Crusher" Kelly. He was someone that probably should have never been a fighter, and yet he was one of the greats. He was even a legend to some. But life has a way of throwing curve balls when it comes to what we should be doing.

A lot has been written about Liam Kelly... most of it not too flattering. Most of it far from the truth, but truth never made a tabloid worth reading. However, after all these years, I wonder how many people knew what really happened or even cared about the truth. I think the true story is much more interesting, even if it doesn't sell newspapers or get as many hits on the internet. And when people talk about legacy, I've always wondered if its built upon the lies we tell or the truth that should be told. For me, legacy should be based on the truth... the cold, dark truth so that people can decide if the man is truly worthy of a legacy.

At the end of the day, that's why I started writing the Rise and Fall of Liam "The Crusher" Kelly. People have the right to know what happened and why. People have the right to make their own judgment and not have it made for them. And the only way to tell a good story... a true story is to start from the beginning. This one is about the making of a fighter.

ROUND 1

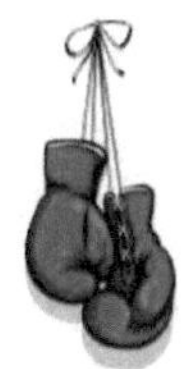

February 17, 2007

The bell rang and the eleventh round finally ended. Both fighters could hardly find their corners, giving a true testament to the war that had been fought that night.   The Arena was electrifying and pulsed at the roar of the crowd... the way it should be in a Light Heavy Championship fight. And it was the perfect atmosphere for George Coghlan. As a Boxing trainer these were the kinds of moments he lived for, especially when he was helping to put his fighter back together for the next round.

He helped Tommy Burns, the number one contender, back to his corner. Tommy was hurt bad. One eye was swollen shut and he could barely stand.   George didn't know for sure if he was going to make out for the final round, but that's where he did his best work. He started talking to his fighter... getting him pumped up for the next round. As the cut man worked on Tommy, George said.

"Alright, listen to me... you're doing good... just three more minutes and you have this thing won."

Tommy was breathing hard. "I have him... one more hook and I got him... he's going down."

"Hey, you don't need to knock him out to win. You got him beat on points. All you need to do is stay away from his right... just keep jabbing and stay away.

"No way, I have him... I can knock him out!"

George lightly slapped him. "Shut up and listen... you try to throw that hook and leave yourself open... that's when he has you... jab and move. You keep away and you win. You keep away by jabbing and moving."

"I am going to knock his ass out."

"Don't be stupid... jab and move."

The bell rang again and the fighters returned to the center of the ring for the final round. George knew his fighter would be champion if he followed his instructions, but ego can be the biggest enemy of a fighter.

Tommy wanted to win by knockout. He wanted the ESPN highlight. He started the round jabbing and moving like he was supposed to… *jab, jab, then move… jab, jab, then move… jab, jab then move!*

He kept doing that until about thirty seconds into the round when he tried to throw a hook. Just like George predicted he left himself open and the Champ floored him with an uppercut. Tommy went down like a bag of rocks. He fell hard and fast. He didn't even try to get up as the count quickly got to ten. George was concerned about his fighter as he lay on the canvas, but he was more angry with him than anything else because he didn't listen and he could have been the new light heavyweight champion of the world. The crowd cheered like crazy over the knockout, but it was like a sucker punch to the ribs for George.

Twenty minutes later all you could hear from the contender's dressing room were men yelling. They weren't trying to console the fighter who lost. They were playing the blame game. Tommy's sponsors and managers from ACM Management were like petulant children trying to figure out who was really to blame for the loss. They didn't really care about the fighter…this was business to them, just a means to make millions of dollars. They were even worse than Don King if that could be possible. Finally, they decided to blame the trainer. George didn't care much for their opinion and as one of the managers said, "You told us that he could be Champion…" George cut him off…

"Let me stop you there…I know that I'm the easiest one to blame, but it's always the fighter who is to blame…they're the ones in the ring. They're the ones giving and taking the punches. What I told you three years ago is that I could make him a champion, if he listened to me. And, if he followed my program and stuck to our strategy in fights "

One of the managers replied. "Are you implying that Tommy didn't listen to you and that's why he lost?"

"Exactly, he was up on the cards…he stuck to our plan until the final and landed more punches…he was more accurate and didn't get knocked down, unlike the champion and then he did something stupid in the last round…he tried to go for a knockout instead of playing it safe and smart."

"It's your job to make him listen."

"No, that's not how it works… the fighter chooses to listen or do it his away. I can't make that choice for him. My influence is only so much. My job is to give instruction, his job is to listen."

One of the sponsor's spoke up. "Do you know how many millions of dollars you cost us tonight?"

George gave him a sarcastic smile. "Again, you have me confused with the one who was actually in the ring. If the fighter doesn't stick to the game plan that the trainer comes up with then 99% of the time he will lose. The only fighters that I trained who didn't become champions were the ones that didn't listen."

The managers and the sponsors didn't like the answer. They couldn't see beyond the dollar signs and truly understand the science of boxing. Finally, one of them replied. "George, you didn't get it done... you're fired. "

He just laughed. "Fine by me... this is a waste of my time anyway!"

One of the sponsors responded. "Don't be so happy, we will be suing you for breach of contract... you didn't make us a champion."

He laughed again, knowing he was actually serious, but he simply replied. "Well then... you can go fuck yourself, I'm done with this horseshit, anyway." George walked out of the dressing room and never looked back, despite the protests from his colleagues who worked the corner with him. At least for now, he was done with boxing and those who tried to corrupt the sport.

A couple of days had gone by and it still hadn't really sunk in. He was fired. George had been fired before. It was nothing new in the boxing industry. Trainers go from job to job. On average a trainer's job will last two to three years with one fighter. Maybe, it will last more than five years, but most jobs were short lived because boxers could be like stuck-up teenager girls, always thinking they could do better. But the one's that hurt the most, were the ones where the boxer never listened and the trainer always got the blame.

These days he drank more than usual. He never drank as much when he was training a fighter as if it was some kind of shadow training regimen with his boxer... when the fighter lived a healthy lifestyle, so did he. And so it was, this particular Monday night that he found himself at a local Irish Pub with his friend Paul, who owned the Holy Trinity Gym, putting away a few rounds of Guinness and Irish whiskey. They laughed about old times. They told the same stories

they had told over the last thirty years.
Finally, Paul asked. "So what are you going to
do now?"

George laughed. "I don't know... I guess
retire. "

"Bullshit... you don't know how to
retire."

"Eventually, I have to. I just turned
sixty-five."

"What... you collect social security and
you think it's time to retire."

"Isn't that the way it's supposed to be?
Besides, I've done enough in boxing."

Paul laughed. "I've known you too long.
There's no such thing as enough. "

George took another shot of whiskey.
He winced at the burning feeling he felt down
his throat. "Maybe, you're right. "

"I Know. So I ask, again, what are you
going to do... try and find another fighter."

"I don't think anybody will take me at
this point. Too much controversy!"

"Well, you can always come by the gym
and work with the fighters there. There's a few
good prospects."

George shrugged at the idea. "I'm too
old to play wet nurse to a bunch of fighters
who are going nowhere."

"I'll bet you that after three days of
sitting around and doing nothing, I'll see you

down there at 6am."

George laughed. " Three days, uh, and what's the bet?"

"Same as usual... a beer and a shot."

George couldn't help but laugh. The sad thing is, he was right. George was too restless and he had to be around boxing. It would probably be more like two days. He replied to Paul. " You know what I really want."

"What?"

"Just one more time, I'd like to discover a fighter who would truly listen to me about strategy and had real talent. The kind of talent that you can't teach... it's just blind instinct and every punch they throw seems too easy. You know, that perfect blend of talent, brains, and heart. "

Paul smiled. "We both know that those fighters are rare... maybe they come along once in a generation and you've only had one in your life time. "

"Yeah...very true. Bobby Lewis... he was a hell of a fighter. But we both know that no boxer is perfect and has at least one or two personal demons they can't shake. "

"I've always wondered how long he could have had the Championship if he never got a taste for coke....I think he could have held on to the belt longer than Joe Lewis."

"Maybe, but before I'm done... I want to find one more fighter like that. Just one more time. Truth is they're probably not out there, but if I could find one that has it all, it would make all of this worth it. "

Paul took a sip of beer. "You sound like a fighter that thinks they have one more fight in them and doesn't know when to hang it up."

"Probably right, but people can get lucky more than once. Hell, George Foreman won the title again at forty-five"

Paul raised his whiskey glass. "Well, here's to that perfect fighter and you better drink up... probably the only thing you'll get out of this deal."

George laughed. Raised his glass and replied. "Knowing how my luck really is... you may be right. "

But the truth is, luck is like lightning... you never know where it will strike. And it can strike more than once. It happens more than we think it does. For what George didn't realize... getting lucky twice wasn't that uncommon. However, would he recognize it again... that was the real question.

ROUND 2

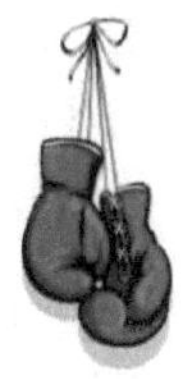

It was one year later and George Coghlan was semi-retired. He didn't try to fool himself, he could never truly get away from the sport so a few days a week he helped out his friend Paul at the Holy Trinity Gym, assessing and working with some of the young fighters that come through. It was just something to do in order to keep busy. On the days he wasn't working at the gym, he took his brother's other season ticket to the local Chicago Cougars Hockey Games, a team in the lowly U.S. Premier Hockey League. It was a Tier 3 hockey league filled mostly with players that would never play in the NHL. It was often called the last stop before retirement. But the games were always fun and fights were never stopped. It gave George and his brother Paul a chance to catch up.

Paul asked his brother. "So are you finally going to retire or pretend to be retired?."

George laughed. "Don't think I could ever be permanently retired... boredom would kill me and at least this way I still get to be a part of the sport."

"Any good boxers at the gym... someone you could work with?"

"Not really... some decent ones, mostly stepping stones for true contenders."

"That's a shame because you need a project... not that I'm not happy to have you with me at these games, but it's weird seeing you so much."

"A project, I've had many over the years, some good, some bad... I don't think I need another one."

His brother laughed. "Who are you fooling... you get bored too easily. That's why you're really at the gym all the time and as much as you like hockey, you don't like having time to go to games... you like watching it in the background as you go over your notes about fighters."

George laughed. "Maybe you're right, but I haven't found anything that peaks my interest."

As he was a finishing his sentence, a fight broke out between two defensemen and in this league, the fights could be the most exciting part of the game. The defensemen from the opposing team started punching first. He got a few shots in, grabbing the other man's jersey to keep his balance, but he didn't make a dent and couldn't get the other guy to go down. Finally, the cougar's defensemen grabbed his opponent's jersey with his right hand, stunning the man that he wasn't really hurt. Then his opponent tried to hit him with an over the shoulder hook. It failed miserably. The cougar's defensemen rolled underneath it to the right, twisting his body just enough to land a devastating uppercut that knocked his opponent, clean out. He fell to the ice like a sack of potatoes. As great as the knockout was, it cost the cougar's defensemen a ten minute major penalty.

There were boos from the home crowd, but George wasn't among them. He was wowed by what he just saw. He said to his brother. "Holy shit, did you just see that?

"Yeah, he knocked him out... it's not uncommon in this league"

"Sure, but it's the way he did it... rolling underneath a right hook and laying him out with just one punch... you can try and teach that but most boxers never learn it effectively, especially heavyweights. That is pure raw talent"

"Uh oh... I've seen that look before... you're never easily impressed. "

"What's the kid's name?"

His brother looked it up in the program. "Liam Kelly... he's from Chicago."

"Well, that kid is a natural, but not at hockey."

When the game was over, George stayed behind while the crowd dwindled out of the small stadium. He told his brother, he would catch up with him later. Most of the players had already showered and left when George talked his way into the locker room and found Liam getting dressed. Liam didn't seem to notice or didn't want to. He was pissed at the outcome of the game, mostly because he didn't get to play anymore after his penalty. George spoke up. "You knocked the shit out of that guy... that was a pretty impressive upper cut"

Liam gave him a strange look. "Thanks, I guess. "

"I haven't seen many fighters, including champions who can throw that punch the way you did....have you ever boxed before?"

"Not really... just messing around at the community center when I was a kid?"

"Where did you learn to throw that punch?"

"I think I saw it in a Bruce Lee movie or something..."

George Laughed at the comment... he thought it was funny because most people usually learn the wrong the moves from movies. Liam asked. "Who are you... some kind of crazy fan?"

"No...not so much... that would be my brother. I'm curious...do you like to play hockey or do you like to fight?"

"I like both."

"But which do you like more?"

Liam smiled. "Fighting."

George nodded in an agreement. "That's what I thought."

"No offense old man, why are you talking to me?"

"Because I'm a boxing trainer and I think with some work, you can be a great fighter in a sport where you don't get sent to the penalty box for doing it. "

"Okay, but I'm a hockey player."

"I don't think that's going to last too long... this league is the last stop of a career. You either play as a teenager to get some experience or you play the end of your career until it's time to do something else. There are no second chances in this league."

Liam stood up. "What do you know of it...look at my size...professional teams look for big guys like me and I put up good stats."

George laughed. "That may be true, but I looked you up and from what I understand you got your shot when you got drafted by St. Louis. Then they kicked you out of their system eight months later and then no team would pick you up even for their farm system. Like I said, this is a last stop league."

"Fuck you, man"

George had to laugh. "Nice, but it won't change anything, this is your last chance at Hockey." George reached into his wallet and got out a business card. He handed it to Liam who hesitated before taking it. Liam didn't really want to. He was at least being nice so the old man would go away. George continued saying. "When you're done with hockey or I should say, hockey is done with you and you still want to fight then give me a call."

"Why?" Liam asked with curiosity.

"Because I don't think you're going to stop fighting and if you do it as a boxer, you won't go to jail for assault. Besides, you can make some good money. More than you will make playing in some two bit hockey league"

"Really!"

"Yeah…really…you have a lot of raw talent and with the right training, Like I said, I think you can be a great fighter and great fighters can make serious money."

Liam finished putting his stuff in his gym back. "How do I know you're legit and this isn't some kind of setup just to make some money off of me in the ring."

"If that were true, then I would be trying to book you for a wrestling event…the sport where you pretend to fight. "

Liam laughed at the comment, but didn't say anything. George continued to try and put his mind at ease. "Tell you what, why don't you get on the internet and look me up…you can decide if I'm legit enough. And if this is something that you want to do…come find me at the Holy Trinity Gym… I'm usually there Monday through Friday in the mornings."

That's all he said. He then turned around and walked out the locker room. Liam stared at the business card for a few moments. He wondered what he could be without hockey. Even he knew that his chances of making it to a better league or even the NHL were slim, but he didn't know what else he could do except work some dead end job and be another bum from the neighborhood if he didn't have hockey. The

Coach leaned out of his office and asked to see Liam and that's when he got pits in his stomach for the first time in his life. Somehow, he knew it was bad news.

On his way home, Liam stopped at the local neighborhood Irish Pub, called Murphy's. It was like the unofficial community center. Everybody knew each other's business and it was never short of old drunks, gamblers, mobsters, and priests. Liam hadn't been in a while, but it didn't matter because nothing ever seemed to change. His friend that he had known since elementary school was working behind the bar that night. His name was William, but for some reason everybody called him Vic. Liam, couldn't remember how he got the name.

Liam sat down at the bar. Vic brought him a tall pint of Guinness, he needed it more than most that night. He said. "You look like shit man…look like you could use a beer…it's on the house."

"Thanks… I think my Hockey career just ended."

"Really, you got cut tonight."

"Yeah and don't think I'm going to get picked up by anybody. "

"Ah, don't' fret mate, there's got to be some team out there that can use a big defenseman or enforcer".

Liam smiled. "I don't know man, some guy I met tonight called it a last stop league. Maybe he's right...I don't have anywhere else to go."

"Sounds like an asshole who doesn't know shit."

"Probably...he was a little strange. Gave me his card and said he was a boxing trainer."

This peaked Vic's interest. He was a boxing fan. "Really...what's his name?"

Liam got out his card. "You keep up with boxing don't you?" Vic nodded yes. "Do you know the names of trainers?"

Vic replied. " I know some." He took a look at the card and saw the name. He was impressed. "Wow, George Coghlan is pretty famous for a trainer... he's trained his fair share of champions."

Liam was shocked. "Really! I thought he was just some old man full of shit."

"Well, all old men are a little full of shit."

Liam laughed. " True."

Vic handed the card back. "This guy is legit. He trained Charlie "Ironman" Waters...he beat Leon Spinks, Ken Norton, and Ali, he was a great fighter for about five years in the late seventies and early eighties."

Liam didn't know who he was, but knew of Muhammad Ali.   But didn't everybody! He knew enough to know that beating Ali meant you were a great fighter so he was impressed. Vic continued. "He trained Bobby Lewis. He was Mike Tyson before Mike Tyson…could knock a guy out with one punch and his fights usually ended in the first or second round." Liam was a little shocked because that sort of thing seemed farfetched.

Liam replied. " So the old man is for real, uh?"

"Oh yeah. If he thinks you can be a boxer… it's worth checking out. I mean, he knows what he's talking about." Liam was more intrigued by the idea. Just because he had always been able to fight didn't mean he thought he could do it as a career. All he had ever cared about when it came to sports was hockey. Ever since he got to hold a hockey stick for the first time or put on a pair of skates and slapped a puck into the net, hockey was the most important thing in his life next to his mother. He finished his pint of Guinness and headed home.

Liam put his hockey gear away when he got home. He thought about throwing it away, but just couldn't do it. He couldn't let go of the idea that he might get another shot and ignored the truth he knew deep down. Hockey was over even though he wouldn't admit it. He was depressed. After All, why wouldn't he be. He had no prospects. He had no career. He was a just another guy from the neighborhood that never made it. So he did the only he could do to quell hos depression that didn't involve alcohol. He just went to bed.

It was 2AM and Liam couldn't sleep. He tried to take his mind off the end of hockey career. What was he going to do now? However, the more he thought about the man he had just met, the more he was intrigued by the idea of becoming a fighter . Still, he couldn't shake the feeling that he was just some old man full of shit. There were a lot of those in his neighborhood and he was used to men embellishing the truth about themselves, but he couldn't stop thinking about it and that's usually the start of something. A professional boxer! Could he really be one, but then again, he liked to fight and was pretty good at it. In Hockey, he was a natural enforcer.

He had an old laptop that barely got on the internet, but he was able to do a Google search for George Coghlan. Sure enough, Vic was right about the old man. He had been in the boxing game for about forty years and had trained a lot champions. That made him an expert to Liam. Maybe it was worth talking him, he thought. He watched some videos of the fighters he worked with. He watched some of Charlie's Waters and a few more with Bobby Lewis. There were more videos of him working with other fighters that he had never heard of, but all of them became champions. There was an ESPN special about George Coghlan working with some of these fighters. It was informative and almost felt like an instructional video. Liam learned a lot by just watching that. The more he watched videos, the more excited he got.

Maybe it would work out or maybe it wouldn't, but he would rather be excited than depressed. And there was plenty to be depressed about when it came to his future. The only thing he had going for him was a crummy bouncer job that went great with his shitty apartment. At this point in his life, what else was he going to do? Liam looked for a smaller gym bag than his hockey bag. It's not like he needed it more. He even checked the closet that was reserved for junk. The apartment was his mother's before she died and there was stuff that had been collecting dust for almost twenty years...stuff that was meant to be forgotten. It was a good place for his hockey gear. It wouldn't be too long before it started collecting dust only to be forgotten. Liam tried to get some sleep, but the agonizing thought of not having much of a future kept him awake. Finally, he just started doing pushups to keep from having to think about everything..

ROUND 3

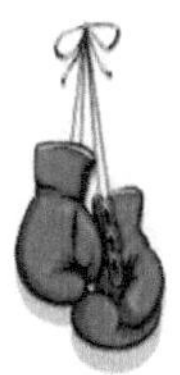

George usually went to the Gym at 6AM. He was normally an early riser and had never gotten out that habit since leaving the Marines over forty years ago. Most of the boxers who trained at the Holy Trinity Gym were there that early trying to get a workout in before they went to their real jobs that put food on the table. By eleven a.m., George had already put in a half day. He was working with a young middleweight who couldn't stay balanced when hitting the heavy bag. It was irritating and he finally responded. "Johnson, for the love of god, what have we talked about… if you don't have balance then you can't put your full power into your punches. You look like you're trying to hop on one leg and throw a punch" George got a piece of chalk from his pocket and bent down to draw an outline of two feet spaced shoulder width apart. "Johnson… put your feet in those outlines and keep them there. Stay within the lines and you will stay balanced. " The young boxer tried and immediately felt more power from his punch. George replied. "See what happens when you have balance. Now, if you step out of the line, then I am going to tie a string around your feet."

Paul, the owner of the gym walked over to George and said. "Hey, some kid is here asking for you. Says he met you last night."

George smiled. "Yep…figured he'd come by."

Paul replied. "Who is he?"

"A new project."

"Oh really, is he a good prospect?"

"We'll see."

"And I thought you were retired. How's that working for you?"

"I'm here when you open Monday through Friday, does it look like I'm retired?" Paul laughed. George responded. "But, I guess guys like us never really retire."

George walked over to the front entrance of the gym and found Liam Kelly waiting for him. The kid took a chance and showed up. Liam said. "Well, I'm here."

"So you are…I guess you looked me up and found out that I wasn't full of shit."

"My friend Vic knew who you were…he said you were legit."

George smiled. " Ah my reputation precedes me."

"I guess. So you trained Big Daddy Carson."

"Yep…he really wasn't a great fighter, but he learned well and became a great fighter."

"What about Don Holyfield."

George laughed. "Well, he was a naturally gifted fighter, but he still had to learn the basics cause raw talent only gets you so far, which brings us to you."

"What about me?"

"If you're here…you're curious to see what you can do, but what I really want to know is how serious you are?"

"I'm here, aren't' I."

"Not good enough. You have to really want to do this…to be here every day…to do the hardest workout you're ever going to have to do and do it without quitting. You're going to have to go through hell! And I am not here to have my time wasted."

Liam paused for a moment. "Will it be worth it?"

"You could be a champion one day so you tell me!"

Liam smiled at the thought. "Really! You think so."

George replied. "Wouldn't be standing here talking to you unless I thought you could. "Plus, it's better to be going somewhere than nowhere and you look like you're going nowhere."

Liam didn't say anything, but nodded and gave him a look as if he agreed with that assessment. And then George asked him. "So are you ready to get started?"

"Yes."

"Good, let's see if that's still true in a week because I wasn't kidding, you're going to go through hell."

Liam laughed. "So you keep saying, I was in the army and basic training for the infantry was pretty hard. "

"Well, I was in the Marines and this kind of training is harder than any boot camp we've been through. You'll just get a little more sleep."

George walked him around the gym and started to explain what they were going to do. He showed him each station that he would be working on. "Now Liam...there are four stations in this gym that will be your world, so to speak, for the next few weeks...the heavy bag, the speed bag, the double end striking bag, and mirrors for shadow boxing. "

Liam looked at one of the rings in the gym. "What about the ring. Don't I get to fight someone?"

"You're not ready for that yet. Just like boot camp, we have to break you down and rebuild you, especially since you have no experience. You have to learn technique first...until then sparing is a waste of time. If you don't know what you're doing, then you'll just hurt yourself."

Liam didn't like the answer. He just wanted to hit someone. But he had been an athlete long enough to know that you had to learn the fundamentals before you could play no matter how boring it might be.

George walked him over to the dressing rooms. "Don't suppose you have any boxing gloves in your gym bag?"

Liam shook his head. "No... just workout clothes."

"Eventually, you will need to get some, but we have gloves around here that you can use." George found a pair that would fit Liam's 6'3" 225 LB frame. Liam was about to put them on when George stopped him. No kid, not yet...gotta get you taped up first. This is the first thing we do when you get here so start getting used to it. It will be weird at first, but after a few weeks, it will feel just as comfortable as a pair of warm socks on a cold Chicago day. "

After getting taped up and doing some stretching, George walked him over the mirrors for shadow boxing. He put Liam in a proper's fighter's stance and moved his hands up in the right position. "Now, take a good look at your stance and where your hands are...this is where you should be at all times when you're not throwing a punch or moving out of the way from one...if you're going to be a fighter, this is your most important position and you always come back to it when you're not hitting or blocking. George showed him how to throw a punch from the position... jabs, hooks, and what became Liam's killer punch, the left cross and then to come back to his stance. Liam was a southpaw so George had to show him the opposite way of throwing since he was right handed, but he also knew that besides Liam's uppercut, if he learned to throw a left cross, it would end most of his fights.   "I know you're not used to this, but this is how you are going to hit from now on."

It felt weird to Liam, but on the other hand, he was used to just wildly throwing punches and hoping they would land on someone's face. Most of the time his punches did hit their mark...he was lucky that way.

George watched for about ten minutes. "Okay, we need to work on your footwork… you keep coming out of position."

Liam replied. "Why, I feel fine."

George smiled. "Alright …let me show something." They walked over to one of the heavy bags. After Liam put on the boxing gloves, George told him to just throw a punch as hard as he could without getting into a position. Liam did it and felt like he hit the bag hard. George replied. "Okay, now get into position I showed you." He tied a leg band around Liam's legs that was about shoulder length apart. It was a boxing tool to help fighters keep their feet in the right position. George said. "Now hit the bag and drive from your legs." Liam hit the bag a lot harder. "See how much power you have when you're in the right position and drive from your legs." Liam smiled. "Get used to hearing that a lot because I will say it over and over like a broken record

For the next half hour they worked the heavy bag and George showed him all the different kinds of punches he could throw. George was impressed. The kid could hit hard and he was strong. All the years of having to stay in shape playing hockey made him strong, but right now, all Liam was, was just a brawler and brawlers didn't become champions. That only happened in the movies.   He wanted Liam to be a boxer with the right technique and skills that could make him go the distance in every fight and not get beat to death in the ring.

Eventually George took him through all the stations. Liam had trouble with the speed bag at first and the double end striking bag made him look silly on his first day because he couldn't seem to land a straight punch. But George saw that he had potential...the raw skills were there and that's all he needed to mold Liam Kelly into a great fighter.

Sometimes a boxing trainer has to be like a drill sergeant. You push your fighter until they think they can't go anymore and then you push even more to see how far they really can go. Everything is about routine. You make a fighter work each station until it becomes second nature... until they can do everything in their sleep. Just like making a soldier, you change their habits, getting rid of the bad ones and making it so that every habit is that of a boxer preparing for a fight. Everything right down to how they sleep, when they get up, what they eat, and most importantly, how they treat their body in order to keep it in peak shape. It's tedious and methodical, and that's why the first four weeks are the most important. It's just like

boot camp. It's not fun, but necessary. Just
like clay for a sculpture, you break them down
and build them up. George told him that
every muscle would hurt, but at the end of it,
he would find the strength that he never knew
he had; George did all of this mostly to see if
Liam would keep showing up.

ROUND 4

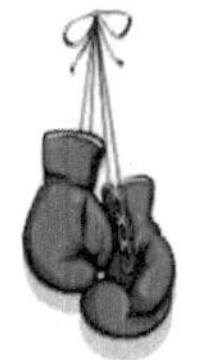

Over the next four weeks, Liam had the same routine. He was at the gym by 7AM and he went through each station until it was becoming second nature. He was getting the hang of the speed bag and hitting the double strike bag didn't feel as awkward after a few weeks. He could hit hard so the heavy bag was never a problem. Every time he hit it, you could hear a faint cracking sound as it rattled backwards. Liam's biggest problem like most fighters starting out was keeping the correct stance. George and Liam spent a lot of time shadow boxing and for the first week he was wearing the leg bands most of the time.

They were inside one of the boxing rings and shadow boxing when George got frustrated. "Fucking Christ...your footwork is horrible. You would think the leg bands would help." It seemed like George was always saying that to fighters.

Liam seemed confused. " I feel fine, why are you complaining."

"Of course you feel fine... but just wait until you actually hit a guy and break a hand because you're off balance."

"I wouldn't know...you won't let me hit someone."

"So you don't break a hand by being off balance. Remember, it's about learning the proper technique. But it doesn't matter at this point, until we solve the problem of your footwork, then you can't start sparing." George walked out of the ring and walked over to the where there was a little stereo system in the gym. Some fighters liked to bring workout music. George had his own playlist. He put a CD into the stereo and grabbed the remote control. As he climbed back into the right, he started to lecture.

"Having the proper footwork... having balance is like the perfect dance. Do you know how to dance?"

Liam seemed confused by the question. "I don't dance. Guys from my neighborhood don't dance."

"Why?"

"I always thought it was for sissies."

George gave him a dirty look. "Really. You know that men who can dance, get laid more."

Liam smirked. "I do just fine with women. I get laid a lot!"

"Maybe that's true, but real men know how to dance. Anyway, if you can dance then you can fight because you have good footwork. And I never realized that until my wife had me take ballroom dancing with her." George pressed play on the remote control and the Australia Folk Song, Waltzing Matilda started playing. It was the perfect song to demonstrate proper footwork. It was essentially a waltz, just like its namesake. George got into a dancing position and asked Liam to take his hands. Liam gave him a dirty look and shook his head "no." George responded. " Come On, this isn't a gay thing, if that's what you are thinking...I will lead and you mimic what I do. Watch my feet."

Liam paused and then reluctantly took George's hands and started to dance with him. There were laughs from the other boxers in the gym. It pissed Liam off, but George told him not to listen, just dance. And so they did. They danced all around the ring. At first it was hard for Liam, he kept stepping on his trainer's toes, but eventually he started to get the hang of it. He kept his eyes on George's feet the whole time, then he was told to look up and close his eyes. That felt weird.

"Liam close your eyes and feel the moves. Yes, I'm leading, but you don't need your eyes to move."

"What is this some kind of Jedi Mind Trick?"

"I don't know what this, but when your eyes have been beaten shut and you can't see anymore, you will have to rely on knowing your footwork to get through the fight. So this isn't so crazy after all! Liam still thought it was weird, but the dancing became easier. It almost seemed natural after twenty minutes of dancing around the ring. They stopped. George played the song again, but this time he put the trainers gloves on and told Liam to dance the same moves and then jab. There was more power in the jabs. He was a little faster too. George told him to keep doing the move, but bob his head a little bit because he was going to throw some punches and wanted to see Liam get out the way.

Liam felt light on his feet and it made it easier to get out of the way. More importantly, his feet were properly spaced. While waltzing wasn't the best way to move in the ring, it showed Liam how dancing could help him with his footwork. George replied.

"See, now doesn't it feel better when you move and punch."

"Maybe, but I still think this is weird."

George laughed. "If ballet can be good for football players then I figure a good waltz can be good for boxers."

"You're not going to make me wear a tutu, are you?"

"Only when you have sloppy footwork. I'll make you wear it when you work the heavy bag. Just keep working on your dance moves. Learn to be to be light on your feet...when you punch...when you have to get out of the way of punch."

Liam still grumbled about the dancing. He sarcastically said. " I better get laid for this."

George smiled. "I can't help you there. I'll only get you a hooker when you win ten fights. You're on your own for the rest."

"I don't need a hooker...I can get laid all on my own."

"Good, that will save me some money."

Liam kept practicing. Finally, after a while, George asked him to stop. "Okay, now that you got that down, I am going to teach you some other dance moves."

Liam gave him a strange look. " I thought I was here to box."

"This is part of the process." George selected another CD. This time it was Disco, straight from the Saturday Night Fever soundtrack. Liam rolled his eyes. He hated disco, but George asked him to get into position. Liam rolled his eyes at the thought and then George started swaying to the beat, trying to do his best John Travolta. He said. "See how I'm moving."

"Yes, and you are doing a terrible job."

"I'm not trying to win a dance contest here. The purpose of this is to show you how to move, but to do the opposite of me. If I move one way, you move the other way."

"You don't want to me to dance the same way you are?"

"Not for the purpose of this drill. You keep your feet straight like before...spaced properly and you move the opposite way. Feel the beat, no matter how ridiculous the music is."

Liam gave him a dirty look, but he started moving. At first it was hard because he followed what George did, trying to learn the dance moves in the process. Eventually he was mimicking the moves, but moving in the opposite direction. After about ten minutes, like before, it didn't feel so weird. He was starting to get it down.   Then George threw a jab at Liam, but missed it because he was moving out of the way at the time. He was surprised at the punch. Liam responded. "What was that?"

"To show you how you can slip a jab with the proper footwork and learning to move opposite of your opponent. Now do you understand the purpose of this drill?"

Liam smiled. It finally made sense There was actually a purpose to dancing in boxing as crazy as that might be. They kept dancing and every once in a while George would throw another jab or even a hook just to see if Liam would be fooled by it. He never got hit once. Finally, George said. "Okay, you're learning how to move out of the way of a punch, but can you throw a counter punch at the same time?" He stopped dancing and put on upper body padding. "Now, what I want you to do is keep dancing, but when I throw a jab or come around with a hook, duck or move out of the way and then throw a body shot or come underneath with an uppercut. It's one thing to not be hit, but good fighters can always counterpunch at the same time."

Liam nodded. "You want me to keep dancing?"

"Of course...never stop moving or you become a sitting target."

"So I should always be dancing to disco music!"

"George laughed. "No, you don't have to listen to Disco. But it's not uncommon to find your own music and be able to move to the beat in your head. We're all inspired by some kind of music. And if you listen to that music long enough, then you can always hear the beat. That's what you want to find and it's the reason I use music to help teach you footwork. Because when you're tired and you think you can't move anymore, you can find that beat...that rhythm and it will get you going again. It doesn't work for every fighter, but if you do find your own music, the beat can save you in the ring. Now show me what you can do."

They continued to move to the music. George threw jabs and hooks at his fighter. Liam didn't get hit once. When a jab came his way, he came underneath with an uppercut. When he saw a left or right hook, he went to the body with pinpoint accuracy to the ribs. Some of the punches were so hard that George could feel them through the padding. At one point they had to stop so George could catch his breath, but he didn't mind that. He was happy...Liam was learning and he even better, he seemed like a natural.

After training was done, Liam walked home. He was only a few miles from the gym. He couldn't get that damn song, Waltzing

Matilda, out of his head. He was humming it all the way back to his apartment. It was annoying, but he didn't forget the moves and kept his feet properly spaced as he was doing a waltz like walk on his way home. Liam passed a gym on his way home, a place that he had never seen before. It had a big store front window where you could see inside. What caught the Liam's eye was a female boxer sparring with a guy. He couldn't help but watch. She was pretty. Plus, she seemed like she knew what she was doing. Liam was fascinated by her.

He had never really thought about female boxers before . He knew they were out there and that girls professionally fighting was an actual thing. But he had never seen a girl box. He stared through the window until she was done sparring. She noticed him looking at her. Normally, it would have seemed creepy and might have made her uncomfortable, but she simply smiled at him. She didn't know why, but it just seemed like the thing to do. Liam smiled back and for a moment they held each other's gaze like they were old friends and had known each other all of their lives. She climbed out the ring and went to the girl's locker room. Liam continued to walk home. He felt pain in his knees and his lower back. It was the same agonizing pain he had, had for years, but he could always dull the pain with the Oxycodone. He was able to buy it cheap from local guys in his neighborhood.

It was the next day. Liam was running a little bit late because he had overslept. He immediately went to the locker room and found George getting tape out. He said to his trainer. "Sorry, I'm late."

George sarcastically replied. " Do I need to get you an alarm clock along with your boxing gear?"

Liam laughed. "It's not like I've been late every day."

"But you shouldn't be late at all. That's the point."

"It won't happen again."

"And you can make up for it by doing an extra hundred pushups and an extra 30 minutes on the jump rope...you can use more practice anyway."

Liam didn't like it, but he didn't argue. "He had been an athlete long enough to know how it worked. When you screw up, you do extra work."

George started to tape Liam's hands. They didn't say anything for a few minutes and then Liam finally asked. "Would you ever train a woman"

"To box?"

"Yeah."

"No."

"You don't think Women should fight?"

"I don't care if they box or not. As far as I am concerned, women can do anything they want to do, especially with their bodies."

"Then why won't you train one."

George shook his head. "Why do you care?"

"I'm just curious."

"Right now, I'm training you...that's all I need."

Liam laughed. "Okay, then don't tell me."

"Fine...when I see a female boxer, I see my daughter...that's all I can see. And the last thing a father wants to see is his daughter get hurt."

Liam was taken back by what he said. He responded. "You have a daughter?"

"Yes I do and I've been told that I have a grandson too."

"You don't know for sure?"

George looked at him and paused for a moment. "I haven't talked to her in about five years, she doesn't like me much, but it doesn't mean I don't still love her and don't want to see her get hurt. "

"Why doesn't she like you?"

"We're here for training...not this conversation and while I am curious to know your fascination about women boxers, we're running late...time for training."

Liam stretched and then went into his gym bag and found the pill bottle. He took a pill and swallowed it with some water. George saw it out of the corner of his eye. He got a little angry and asked. "What did you just take?"

Liam was surprised by the question. "Just a pain killer"

"Like what?"

"Oxycodone."

George gave him a dirty look. "Why are you on that shit?"

"Because my knees and my lower back hurt."

"Did you start taking it when you started training with me?"

"No...,been taking it off and on for the past few years."

George held out his hand. "Give me the bottle...you don't need that shit."

"Fuck off man...what's the big deal!"

"The big deal...you don't need opiates for the pain. You can take care of yourself naturally. It starts with the right diet, proper stretching...plus massages and rub downs."

"It's not like I take one every day."

"That's not the point. The quickest way to ruin your career is to get addicted to pain killers and that's why trainers have a system...we regulate everything because your body is a temple. Remember that. "

"Got it...my body is a temple."

"Say it again."

Liam shot him a dirty look, but George wanted to make sure he understood it. Liam replied. "My body is a temple." George took the bottle of pills and went to a toilet in the locker room so he could flush the pills. He made sure nobody could use them. Liam asked as he came back into the room. "So what do I do if I'm in pain."

George went to one of the cabinets and found the item he was looking for. He put a bottle of Epsom Salt in Liam's gym bag. "Pour two cups of that in a bath and then soak for half an hour. It will help with the pain." Liam wasn't quite sure whether to believe him or not, but he didn't argue. He simply got on with his training.

Later that evening Liam went to work. He was still bouncing at The Lucky Mick, a strip joint with three stages and half of dozen private rooms. That made it one of the high end clubs in his neighborhood. It stayed busy and very rarely had a quiet night. Liam could always get hours there when he needed them. The owner had always had a thing for his mother when she was alive. Liam figured, he loved her enough to take care of her, but never enough to live with her. He had a too many business interests in Chicago and there probably weren't any women that could make him leave and start over. Liam's mother cocktailed there before she got sick, but the owner never allowed her to dance even when she wanted to. It was his way of keeping his mother pure in some weird fucked up way.

Usually when Liam worked, he had to break up a couple of fights or punch some guy for getting too friendly with a dancer. And the owner liked having him work because he was the best fighter among the bouncers and most customers knew enough not to argue when

Liam had to throw them out or get physical. This night started out like most nights, but about halfway through his shift a few guys started to cause a scene near the main stage. At first, they were just arguing over money; something about who was paying for the drinks. Pretty much any argument over money graduated to a fight and that's what happened to these guys. One guy didn't put enough money in to cover the drinks or a lap dance...another guy pulled a gun, which, believe it or not, was not uncommon for the Lucky Mick.

Liam rushed in and immediately punched the guy with the gun, knocking him to the ground. The gun fell out of his hand. One of the other bouncers grabbed it.   Liam looked up at the guy who didn't have enough money and the gun was pulled on. He was stunned and didn't say anything. He knew the man and he had not seen him ten years, but still he knew him as if he had seen him yesterday. It was his father. It took a moment, but finally, the old man recognized his son. He replied. "Liam...wow, you've grown up."

Liam was not exactly happy to see him and it showed in his tone of voice. "Yeah, ten years will do that to a kid. What the fuck are you doing here?"

"Just here to have a good time."

"I meant in Chicago...thought you went out west or something."

"I've been all over America the past ten years, making deals and trying to earn a living. Just happen to be back in Chicago. But boy, it's good to see you." He tried to give his son a hug, but Liam pushed him away. The fight had been broken up and the men involved were escorted out. Liam walked his father towards the door. There were no exceptions at The Lucky Mick, you fight, you get tossed out. Liam's father didn't really argue, he had been in enough strips joint over the course of his life to know how it works. Even though he didn't start the fight, he didn't make excuses and let his son throw him out of the joint. He was more excited to see his son. As they got to the door, his father responded. "I never expected to see you working in a place like this, I thought you'd be playing professional hockey somewhere."

Liam replied. "I did for a while, but my career ended...guess I was never good enough."

"Bullshit, I remember watching you play...you had the right stuff kid."

"Not really or I'd still be playing."

"What happened?"

"Doesn't matter."

"Okay, we don't have to talk about it if you don't want to. So, how's your mother?"

Liam got angry. The son of a bitch didn't know about here. And as far as he was concerned, his father didn't have the right to ask, but he answered the question with as much disdain as he could muster. "She's dead...died when I was seventeen."

His father seemed shocked. "I didn't know."

"Why would you, you just up and left, not that you were any prize when you were there."

His father could tell he was angry and wanted to hit him. He was annoyed, but didn't press the issue, He just let his son hate him. It was easier that way, but he did reply to Liam. "I'm sorry to hear that and you have every right to be mad at me. But I did love your mother. I never stopped. I just couldn't handle being married. Some men aren't cut out for it."

Liam was boiling over with anger at this point. He clenched his fist and it took every bit of willpower not to punch his father out. But there was also so much he wanted to say to the old man. He wanted him to know how much he had hurt his mother, how much he had let them down, and to make him understand how much of a piece of shit he really was. However, the words weren't there, There were only two that dripped from his tongue. "Fuck you," Liam replied. "Any love you had for her was written all over her face pretty much every day and when she needed you the most, you fucking left because you're nothing but a selfish asshole."

His father didn't say anything for a moment. His son was right for the most part. But he did respond. "I probably deserve that."

"Goddamn right, you do. If I see you in here again, you're leaving on a stretcher. In the meantime, go fuck yourself."

His father didn't respond. Nothing he could would get his son to stop being angry at him. He still loved Liam...he was his son...that kind of love doesn't go away unless you never had it before, but he had always loved his son. He had loved being a father and getting to teach his son different things like hockey or baseball, teaching him about American muscle cars, and even how to pick a winner at the track. He had fun with his son when Liam was a kid. But he loved having a good time more and being home at a reasonable hour like a responsible adult always seemed too hard. And in the end, it just made him an all-around disappointment to his wife and his kid...the kind of man who was hard to forgive.

The owner of the club walked out of his office. He had seen everything on the security cameras in his office. He found Liam at the bar and said. "Lad, are you okay."

Liam thought it was a strange question. After all, he was just doing his job. "Yeah, I'm fine...why?"

"Why...you just had to throw your father out of the joint...a man you haven't seen in ten years."

"Just doing my job. No big deal."

"If you say so, but if I ran into the man who ran out on me and mother, I'd probably kill him."

Liam chuckled. "He's just another asshole customer. It doesn't matter if I haven't seen him in ten years, I moved on with my life, Mick."

Mick replied. "Okay, but if you need anything...even if it's just to get drunk or a pharmaceutical escape, it's on the house."

"Thanks, I'll let you know. "

Mick smiled. "Honestly, I thought he was dead...or at least hoped he was for you and your mother's sake, god rest her soul." He walked off, but then turned around and said. "If you want him dead...that can be arranged too." Liam smiled...the thought had crossed his mind. It was never hard to make someone disappear in his neighborhood.

ROUND 5

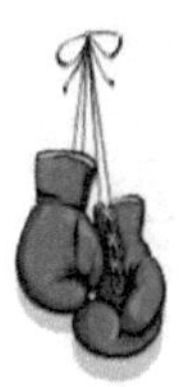

    A few days had gone by since the incident at the club. Liam tried to put it out his mind, but it was hard not to think about it. Seeing his father had brought out feelings that had been dormant for years. However, he went on with his usual routine... that's all he could do. George was watching his workout and timing it.   Liam finished his speed bag workout and caught his breath. He finally asked. "So when do I get to start sparring. "

    George laughed. "When I think you're ready, but you've definitely improved on the speed back so you're getting there. "

    "I can't learn if I'm not hitting someone."

    "Maybe, but until you've mastered all of this...you're not ready for the ring."

    "What...I've gotten pretty good at these stations."

"Pretty good is not the same as mastering it. "

Another fighter as walking by and overheard the conversation. It was Victor Alverez, 18 - 0, and ranked 5th in the Cruiserweight division. He was a good fighter and definitely better than Liam Kelly , even at a lower weight and being from a lower division. And even though it seemed he was all talk, he could back it up, especially in the ring... one of the main reasons he was undefeated. He said. "Hey Coghlan, let him spar, don't be a hard ass. He can spar with me. I'll give him a few lessons."

"Victor, go back to what you were doing...the kid isn't ready, yet, especially against you. "

Liam replied. "Come on, let me do it...I can take him."

Victor laughed. "Take me...please, I'll drop you before you ever got a punch in. But I'm willing to show you what a real fighter can do." He started laughing as he walked off.

George gave Liam a dirty look. "You're not ready to spar with a professional fighter."

"Why not...I'll wear head gear."

"Look it takes most fighters about 3 or 4 years of training to really take on a professional fighter and while I don't think it will really take you that long... a few weeks of training doesn't make you ready. Now, let's get back to shadow boxing. " Liam was angry. He felt like it was an insult not to let him spar, but he wasn't ready to question George yet. With all the training he was putting in, he became more and more excited about becoming a fighter. He wasn't sure at first, but all that changed when he started seeing his potential, he didn't want to piss off the guy who offered to train him so he didn't say anything. But it was hard because he had been fuming the past the few days after seeing his father.

George went to the office to get something. Paul asked him. "How's the kid coming along?"

"He's getting there…he seems to be learning fast, but still having problems with his footwork, making his jab not as powerful as it could be."

"Then why not let him spar."

"You too, uh."

"I'm just saying…see what he can do with a real fighter.

"Because, I want what we're doing to be blind instinct before we spar. Another month and we should be there."

"I would let him spar and see what he can do now."

"And that's why you just manage the gym and I'm the trainer."

"Paul gave him a dirty look. "I know boxing more than you give me credit for."

"You're right, but since, I've actually trained champions, I'll stick with my own advice. "

George walked out of the office and saw that Liam was not where he left him. He found him in one of the rings about to start sparring with Victor Alverez. He got mad and rushed over to the ring. "Liam, what the hell are you doing, I told you, no sparring, yet, especially with him." Liam was angry. "I'm not in here for practice...this is a fight and I am going to kick his ass."

George gave him a sarcastic look. "Oh, okay, you definitely shouldn't do that. You don't fight like a common thug in here...you fight as a professional."

Liam stared at him for a moment. Look, he insulted my mother."

"For fuck sake, what are you in grade school...who cares...ignore him."

"In my neighborhood, you never insult someone's mother or you get an ass whooping. Mothers are a sacred thing." That was true. In a predominately Irish neighborhood, Mothers were looked upon with reverence. They were tough and endured more than most, usually from deadbeat husbands who beat on them, sometimes just for sport It was common and being a very Catholic neighborhood, divorce was never an option. So Mothers were treated with respect and to insult them would be like insulting the mother of Christ herself. It may not have been rational, but love and respect aren't always logical. We just accept the fact that they exist.

George responded. "Alright, fine you want to act like children, then do it… but if you're going to fight or spar or whatever the hell you're doing then do it right." He helped Liam with his boxing gloves and then his head gear. "He's faster than you are so keep moving your head and working your jab. Keep dancing, just like I taught you, Also, keep going for the body. This will keep him from knocking you on your ass." Liam didn't like hearing that and gave George a dirty look.

The two fighters met in the center of the ring and Victor immediately started punching him…jab, jab, jab…jab, jab, jab! George was right , he was faster. Liam kept moving his head trying avoid the punches. He landed a few jabs himself. But Victor was too fast and moved out of the way of most of them. Liam was able to land a few body shots too, but Victor seemed unfazed. The first round went by fast. Liam was pissed that he couldn't seem to do anything and to make matters worse, he had to listen to Victor run his mouth about how bad he was as a fighter.

George gave Liam a few sips of water and said. "Okay...you were behind during the entire round."

Liam replied. "I couldn't get enough space to land anything."

"That's cause a good fighter knows how to stay away or come inside so you can get an accurate punch. What you do is create space...push him and then throw two jabs and a left hook. "

The second round started. It started the same way with Victor jabbing and moving out of the way before Liam could hit him. Finally, about thirty seconds in, Liam pushed off, threw two jabs and then his left hook. It shook Victor, but didn't stop him. He kept jabbing and landing punches while moving out of the way before Liam could land anymore punches of his own

Most of the round went that way until Liam saw an opportunity. He pushed Victor into one of the corners, jabbed twice to the head and then put his full power into a punch to Victor's ribs. Victor started to go down. He couldn't breathe and before he saw it in time, a left hook came around and put him on the mat.

The whole gym who had been watching was shocked. You could hear the jeers from the crowd. Victor was beyond mad and tried to get up so he could knock Liam out, forgetting every boxing rule in the process, but he was hurt too badly. There was a sharp pain in his ribs and trying to get up made breathing even harder. He did manage to pull himself up by use of the ropes. Liam was about to take another swing and one more probably would have knocked Victor out, but it didn't happen.

George immediately jumped into the ring to stop the sparring session. It was clearly over. Liam and Victor's blood boiled over and they wanted to keep fighting. George held his fighter back as Victor was cursing at him in Spanish and being pulled back by some of the other boxers   George said to Liam. "Alright, it's over." Liam tried to get past him to continue the fight. "No sir...you won and we don't kick a man when he's down, no matter how much of an asshole he is. This is supposed to be a sparring session, not a street fight, " He got Liam to his corner and calmed him down. Victor was helped out of the ring and examined by his trainer.

George was getting Liam's gloves off when Paul motioned for him to come to the office. George asked about Victor and Paul chuckled. Well, the kid broke his rib. How about that!"

George was shocked. "Really!"

"Yep...I thought we were going to get lucky and it was only cracked, but nope...it's broken."

"I'm sorry about that."

"Why... you're fighter did great."

"You're not mad!"

"Hell no and it's like I tell every fighter that comes in here. You step inside that ring, you risk getting beat to hell and that's why you prepare and train hard for each battle. Both of them made their choice and assumed the risk."

"Well, I would be if my fighter got beat by a beginner."

Paul laughed. "I'm sure Victor's pissed, but I'm not...he underestimated your fighter. And speaking of...I can see why you chose to work with him....a lot of raw talent there. It's time for him to start fighting for real including sparring. "

George sighed. "He's not ready."

"I disagree and I just made a decision.... If you're going to train here then what's his name..."

"Liam Kelly"

"Then Liam Kelly should represent the Holy Trinity Gym in the All Chicago Boxing Tournament next month."

"No way… he needs at least 6 more months of training and honing his craft before he faces any real fighters."

Paul laughed. "I get being cautious, but this is an amateur tournament…he's good enough to beat most of the guys in the tournament right now. And before you say he's not ready…you have four weeks to get him ready. "

"I understand what you're saying, but I want to do this right…take my time and train him properly."

Paul gave him a dirty look. "What is he…24…25, which means he has about four or five years left in his prime. If you take the four years that it really takes to train a fighter then he will miss his prime years and his carccr would over before it's gets started. You don't have that kind of time."

"I was thinking more like two years."

Paul gave him a dirty look. "But how long before he realistically gets a title shot…if he ever gets one. I'm just saying… put him in the tournament and see what he can do."

"If he starts before he's finally ready, then he'll lose and may never get a title shot. He'll be just another fighter."

Paul sighed. Is this about him or you."

"What are you talking about?"

"You don't want him to be another Bobby Lewis and you don't want to the one to fail him by rushing him too early...is that it?"

"Of course I don't want him to be Bobby Lewis, what a trainer would want that?"

"True, but you still think it was your fault, when I reality when it was always his fault. You've said time and time again, that when a boxer doesn't listen to his trainer, he will lose."

"Yes, I say that, but the other side of that truth is, it's just as much our fault as a trainer if we can't get our fighter to really listen and follow a plan.

Paul took a sip of coffee. "You can't control everything with your fighter...he's still the one in the ring. And you can't hold a fighter back because of your own fears. "

"What are you, my mother?"

Paul laughed. "Maybe someone needs to be since Alice died, God rest her soul. All I am saying is let him fight in the tournament for the Gym."

"And if I don't want to?"

"George...I love you brother, but don't make me tell you to go to another gym...don't make me be that guy. I want Liam Kelly to represent the Holy Trinity Gym in that tournament."

George and Paul had been friends for a long time... about three decades. He didn't want to put Paul in that position, but he also didn't want to rush a good fighter. He didn't want his talent to be wasted by fighting him too early . He had seen too many fighters ruin their careers that way. But, he also knew that he couldn't hold him back either . Liam Kelly had too much talent not to be fighting in the ring. It was a Catch 22 but George knew the ultimate truth about someone Like Liam Kelly...fighters have to fight. He reluctantly agreed with Paul, Liam Kelly would represent the gym in the All Chicago Boxing Tournament.

George found Liam in the locker room getting cleaned up. Liam could tell that his trainer was not happy and figured it was because of what he did. He asked. "Have I been kicked out?"

George was surprised by the question. "No, why would you think that?"

"I just hurt another fighter."

George laughed. " Yeah, you did, but you're not in trouble for that."

"Is Alverez okay?"

"You broke two ribs...he's going to miss his next fight."

"Shit...man, I'm sorry."

"Don't apologize, you did great. If it had been a real fight, we would have gone home early with a big payday. You weren't perfect, but there's definitely things we can work on. Also, have some good news...sort of?"

"If I'm not in trouble and its good news, why do you look pissed."

George laughed. "Yes, but it's good news for you. The owner wants you to represent the gym at the All Chicago Amateur Boxing Tournament and in case you're wondering...that's a big deal.

Liam smiled. "Holy Shit...for real."

"Yep."

"But you don't want me to do it?"

George sighed. "It's not that I don't think you could do well and maybe even win it. You're just not as ready as I would like you to be."

"But I have the talent to be there, right?"

"Yes, you do. But talent and skill aren't the same thing. Talent can make you lucky in the ring, but skill is what wins fights. And that's what I want you to have before your first fight."

Liam put his gloves in his bag. "Do you think I can win and be honest?"

George paused for a moment. "Not on your own, but yes, I think you can win...if you do what I tell you and if you stick to a plan. You can be a common brawler and probably get through the first two rounds, but to win, you got to have a plan and it will change with each fighter."

Liam replied. "I can do that... I will do whatever you tell me to do."

"Alright, I'm still not crazy about this, but if you still want to do it, then I'm in. "

"Liam smiled and George responded. "Oh, you may be smiling now, but I'm going to work your ass off over the next few weeks. No fighter of mine will be unprepared for this tournament."

Liam couldn't stop smiling. He was finally going to gct to fight someone as a professional boxer. George started to walk out of the locker room, but then turned around. His curiosity got the better of him. He asked Liam. "Why did you really get into a fight with Alverez... it can't be just because he said something about your mother...what really happened? I mean, you have been pissed the past few days about something."

"What does it matter?"

"I'm curious and I want to know if it's going to be a problem in the future. When you're angry, you don't think straight."

Liam didn't say anything for a moment, trying to decide if he really wanted to tell George. After all, it had nothing to do with boxing. Finally, he spoke. "I ran into my father the other night... hadn't seen him in ten years. He ran out on my mother and me when I was fifteen."

George was a surprised. "Oh...I guess, I haven't asked about your family."

"There's not much to say. Father was a drunken asshole who cared more about having a good time than his family. He always had some scheme going to make money, which led my mother to work long hours just to make enough so we wouldn't starve. And the last thing he gave my mother was a drug problem. She died two years later from a drug overdose while working as a cocktail waitress at the same club I'm a bouncer in... pretty fucked up, uh!"

George shook his head as if he couldn't believe it. He said. "Yes, it is, but nothing I'm not used to. I'm Boston Irish Catholic and in my neighborhood, domestic abuse was common too Nobody got divorced. And my father was no prize either. You know how I

learned how to fight, by defending my mother
and kid brother when the old man got drunk
and pissed and started whaling on us. And I
never remember him having an honest job.
Eventually, it got him killed. He tried to rip
off a drug dealer in the neighborhood and
then got gunned down in the middle of the
street. The sad thing is, I don't remember ever
shedding a tear for him."

Liam chuckled. "Sounds like our
fathers would running buddies."

George Laughed. "Probably...low-life's
tend to stick together. I'm sorry you had to
deal with what sounds like a huge son of a
bitch."

"He definitely is, but I guess I shouldn't
let it bother me so much."

"It's hard not too... he is your father and
I suppose on some level you're supposed to
love him, but I personally never believed that.
The only thing I know for sure is we can't
truly move on until we learn to forgive and
forget. "

"Forgive the son of a bitch... that
sounds like horseshit."

"I know it does, but it works if you can
do it and then forgetting will be the best that
can happen to you. I hadn't given my father a
thought in over thirty years, until I just
mentioned him to you. You do what you want,

but don't let him affect you boxing... that's when the fucker truly ruins your life. That's about the only advice I can give you on the matter."

George turned around and left the room. He left Liam to think about it, but he wasn't convinced. However, he couldn't stop thinking about what George had said as he walked home. Even when he passed the gym with the big window in front where the women boxers trained. He didn't linger this time...only briefly looked up to see if she was training that night. She was and he smiled when he saw her, but not even she could replace his consuming thoughts about a deadbeat father who never deserved a second thought. And that's when Liam knew, forgetting would be harder than forgiveness.

ROUND 6

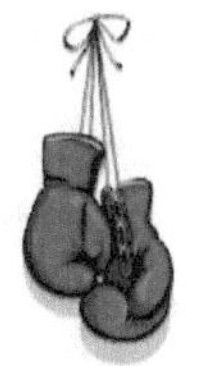

The tournament was always popular in Chicago. Thousands would show up to the Aragon Ballroom in Downtown Chicago for ten days of boxing with fighters from all weight divisions. It was a chance to see fighters that could become champions one day. Sixteen fighters in each division would compete until there was a winner and while most of them were simple street brawlers trying to be a professional boxer, every year there were always a few that would emerge and turn into decent fighters. It was always chaotic the first day with over a hundred fighters trying to get checked in. It made the dressing rooms even more crowded as fighters were waiting to get their first fights out of the way.

The last few weeks seemed like a blur now. He ate, slept, and breathed boxing except for the hours he had to put in at the

Club. He had never done as much training for anything. He had never been as tired or had more muscles on is body hurt. George had to get him ready quick. Some might think that he was pushing his fighter too hard, but there was a method to his madness. George broke Liam down at a faster pace and built him back up even faster, but by the time there were done Liam could master every station and hardly be hit during sparring sessions. Liam learned quickly and his form started to look nothing like a brawler. George was proud of him. He still worried that he wasn't ready to be inside the ring, but that's natural when a trainer cares about his fighter. There wasn't anything more he could with Liam and that's what he told him a few days ago when he said the training was done and he had two days off.

So here they were, a fighter making his debut and a trainer getting one more chance to get it right from the beginning. As Liam was getting ready in the dressing room, George went to find out who he was going to fight first. As he was making his way to the front of the Ballroom with the brackets for every weight division, he ran into an old friend. Here name was Priscilla and her late husband had been one of the best boxing promoters in the country. He had promoted a lot of fights for George back in the old day. Priscilla took over the business when he died and while it may have been unusual for a woman to do boxing promotion in a male dominated sport, she had made a quite a name for herself.

She smiled when she saw George. It had been too long she had seen him, a few years she guessed.   "George Coghlan, where have you been... you don't keep in touch," she said with a thunderous boast. " He chuckled. "I'm not ducking you...I've kept busy with my retirement."

"Oh, you are retired, uh... is retirement going down to the Holy Trinity Gym almost every day to work with fighters."

"I just help out...I'm not training anybody." He didn't want her to know that he had another fighter until they got through the tournament and knew what Liam could really do."

Pricilla smiled. "That's not what I hear."

"People talk a lot of bullshit around here, you shouldn't believe everything"

"Oh...so you don't have a fighter in the tournament?"

George was taken back a little bit. "Now where did you hear that?"

"My company is doing the promotion for the tournament...I saw your name on the list of trainers and fighters."

"I shouldn't be surprised."

"Why didn't you say anything?"

"Because I don't know what he can really do...that's why we're here."

"You must see something in him or else, you wouldn't take the time to train him when you're supposed to be retired. Is he any good?"

George smiled. "He will be. I think he can be one of the best, but we're a long way from promotions."

"Okay, I won't say anything, but you should know...this tournament might already be won in the heavyweight division....there's a new kid, they say hits like George Foreman and take somebody out with just one punch. If you're boy makes it to the final...that's who he'll probably be fighting."

George laughed. "You haven't seen what my fighter can do."

"I did hear something else...like he sparred with Victor Alverez and broke two of his ribs and that's why his next fight got canceled."

George Laughed. "I love rumors too."

"Don't try to deny it...I hear everything when it comes to boxing in Chicago."

"And like everybody else, you will just have to wait and see what happens, but don't think this thing is one, just yet, I thinks folks are going to be very surprised who wins the heavyweight division,   That's all George needed to say. Priscilla could tell that George saw something special in his new fighter and that she should be on the lookout. George's instincts were always good. He knew how to find champions. He knew how to make a good fighter...always did.

George went back to the locker room and started taping Liam's hands. "Apparently, your reputation precedes you,"

Liam look surprised. "What does that mean?

"Apparently, your little stunt with Alverez has gotten around. A promoter was asking me if it was true."

"I didn't say anything."

George laughed. "Wasn't worried about you, but it was bound to get out what really happened. But that's a good thing for you. Folks will be curious and want to come see you fight.

"Cool, I bet Alverez is pissed."

"I wouldn't worry about it...you pissed him off the moment you broke his ribs and made him look like a chump. Now back to business, I found out who you are fighting."

"Who?"

"You're fighting a guy named Jack Hansen."

Liam got excited about knowing who his first opponent would be. " Is he any good?"

"He's just street brawler. Rarely jabs and goes for the big punch, but he has a good right hook. He knocked a lot of kids out that way when he was in Golden Gloves. But you can beat him. Even now, you have more skill than he does"

"What do I do?"

"You're going to move around and work your jab. While he is swinging for the fences trying to knock you out, you're going to wear him down and eventually you will make your move."

"Okay."

George smiled. "You nervous."

"Should I be?"

"Maybe a little. Like some boxer once said, every fighter has a plan when they enter that ring until the first time they get hit and then it goes right out the door. The trick is trying to remember your plan as you're getting hit. That's what we are going to work on tonight."

Liam smiled. "You think I can win."

"You have too much talent not to win. As long as you don't act stupid and try to knock him out with one punch, then you'll be fine."

Liam was a little nervous. He had learned a lot over the past couple of months, but in many ways he was just a street brawler. Even he knew if he kept over thinking everything, he would lose. But he also knew he could hit and he just needed one good punch. He took a few deep breaths and tried to everything out of mind. Forty-five minutes went by and it was his time to fight. The walk to the ring seemed to take too long, but that was just Liam's nerves. Big Jack Henson was already in the ring and he definitely looked like someone that you didn't want to meet in a dark ally.

George got Liam to move around on the balls of his feet and get the blood flowing. The fighters went to the center of the ring and listened to the ref go over the rules. The fights were only six rounds, but with amateur fighters a lot of unethical stuff would happen so the rules were needed even more.

Vic had just finished pouring a beer when he started looking around for the TV remote, he finally found it underneath bar next to the bar double barrel shot gun. He changed the channel from the Chicago Blackhawks game to the Fights. One of the local sports channel was broadcasting the tournament." One of the guys started to complain. "Hey Vic, we were watching the game, what gives?"

"Don't get pissed. The Blackhawks are going to lose anyway…they suck."

"Maybe, but there's nothing else to watch."

"Yeah there is, the All Chicago Boxing tournament…our boy Liam is fighting in it. His fight up right now."

Another guy sitting around the bar spoke up. "You mean Liam Kelly."

Vic replied. "Yep."

"I didn't know he was a boxer."

"Just started, making his debut tonight."

"Fucking eh! About time he started fighting professionally. The way he beats the shit out of people, might as well get paid for it." Vic and the guys started laughing, They all agreed because if you ask anyone of them who the best fighter in the neighborhood, they'd all tell you, Liam Kelly,

The Fight was about to start and so they met at the center of the ring. The ref started talking "Alright, No rabbit punches, no kidney punches, , watch the low blows, and in case of a knockdown, you go to the corner I tell you to. Do you understand these rules." Both fighters nodded yes. "Now put your hands up and touch gloves." Hanson said to Liam. "I'm going to knock you out Motherfucker."

Liam just stared at him with the intensity of a man made of stone and didn't say a word. George replied. Good job. That's exactly what you're supposed to...don't say a thing...let your hands do the talking.

Before the bell rung, Liam closed his eyes and did the Catholic cross...he was ready to go now."

The bell rang. Finally, it was time to fight. Liam with his hands up, met Jack Hanson in the center of the ring. Immediately Jack threw a wild punch and nailed Liam, but he was unfazed. There it was, the first hit, but he remembered the plan. He hit back...jab, jab! Jack threw another wild punch, but Liam ducked and jabbed again. This is how the first round mainly went. Liam just kept throwing his right jab... .jab, jab, then he moved out of the way...jab, jab and he moved again. Jack kept throwing big punches and for the most part Liam was able to get out of the way. Getting his jab inside for a clean shot became harder. Finally, another big hook caught Liam just right and he slipped and fell. He wasn't hurt and he got up by the count of two, but it was still scored as a knockout. The round ended a few seconds after he got up.

Liam had one small cut on his cheek, but nothing too serious. When he got back to his corner, he yelled "Fuck, I fell down."

George said as he worked on him and gave him a sip of water. "Don't worry about it. You still have this guy. He's getting winded. Take a look at him, see how he's breathing heavy"

Liam looked and nodded to confirm. "I can't get my jab in there enough. He keeps swinging wildly."

George made him stand up. "Here's what you're going to do. When he swings that right, come underneath and hit him in the ribs and then bring your left around and hit him square in the face. Go to the body and then go to the head. Okay, go to the body

and go to the head. Keep doing that. He so
winded that after a few times of being hit in
the ribs... your left will knock him out."

The second round started. Jack
Hanson came out swinging big like before.
Liam did what George said. As Jack came
around with that right, he ducked, came
underneath, and hit him in the ribs on the
left side. Then he threw a left hook to the face.
Jack was stunned, but quickly gathered
himself. He came around with a right hook.
Liam did the same, he ducked, hit him in the
ribs on the left side and then a left hook to the
face. Jack almost went down after that. His
ribs were severely bruised. He had to pause
for a moment and gather himself, but he kept
fighting. It wasn't over yet. Jack tried to
protect his left side, but he thought he saw
an opening and swung that right hook again.
Liam ducked, cracked his ribs this time with
his right and then came around with a
devastating left hook. Jack's knees buckled
and he went down fast.

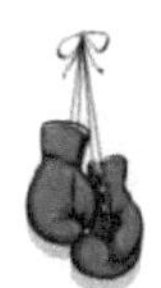

Vic and the guys around the bar started cheering when Liam knocked the guy down. It was so loud inside, that people on the street passing by could hear them. The ref started counting. It was slower than it should be, but didn't matter. Jack Henson didn't even try to get up and beat the count. He just crouched in pain until the ref said ten The guys in the bar watched as Liam jumped up in celebration, realizing that he just knocked him out. It was only thirty seconds into the second round. Henson just sat there stunned. He had more experience and thought he was the better fighter because Liam hadn't been doing this for very long. He just couldn't believe it. Liam walked to help him up along with his trainer. Maybe it was the hockey player in him, but you always show respect towards your opponent by shaking his hand or helping him up especially in the face of defeat.

Liam didn't have to fight again for a couple of days. His trainer was proud to say the least. The first fight was in the books...the first battle done. He wanted Liam to feel excited, but he knew from experience that the road only got harder on the way to the top.   George just told him to go home and relax as much as possible, but he was too pumped. The excitement he felt after winning his first boxing match was the same feeling he had when he scored his first goal as a professional hockey player even if it was in some second rate division that most fans never cared about.

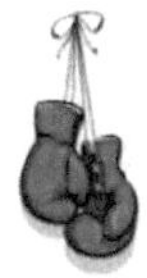

Liam went to the bar for a celebratory Guinness. He didn't know anybody had been watching and when he walked in, he was created to a hero's welcome. Everybody cheered when he walked and when he sat down at the bar, there were so many pats on the back that he lost count. His neighborhood never had heroes, mostly bums and lowlifes so any small victory was like a victory for the neighborhood. It felt good, even if it was only one victory in an amateur tournament. After a few pints, he went home, but he simply couldn't sleep so he worked out and watched clips of some of classic fights on the internet to see how the great ones did it. He had never paid attention to boxing until George Coghlan walked into the locker room that night. He had never seen one of the famous fights between Ali and Frazier or Tyson and Holyfield. He stayed up most of the night watching clips. It was an education in every sense of the word. He needed it because now he was a fighter. With his first fight out of the way he was finally a professional boxer.

ROUND 7

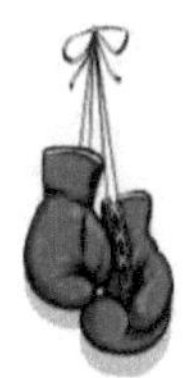

He wasn't due back to the ballroom for a couple of days. He didn't have to fight until the next day, but he just had to be around it. One fight and he was hooked. All he wanted to do was box or train for a match now. The feeling was electrifying and as much as he loved hockey, he couldn't remember if had the same feeling like the one he had now.   He went up to the Aragon ballroom on his day off to watch some of the other fights. To his surprise, he found George sitting in the stands watching one of the heavyweight fights.

George responded when he walked up. "Aren't you supposed to be at home getting some rest?"

Liam smiled. " I couldn't sleep...too excited and I wanted to watch some of the fights. What are you doing here?"

"My job...scouting the other fighters. Right now, I'm watching the guy you're going to face in the next round."

Liam looked surprised. "I thought I was fighting someone named Big Daddy Johnson?"

"You are, but I'm talking about the round after that."

"I haven't even won the next round."

"You will...I'm going to teach you how to beat the guy by the second round. Trust me, he won't be difficult. I hate to use the word forgone conclusion, but trust me, you don't have anything to worry about. "

"And I guess, you already know who's going to win the fight we're watching?"

George smiled. "Yep. And he's going to do it in about thirty seconds."

Liam was curious. "How do you know?"

"Experience! The fighter is named Quenton Hopkins... he's got the fastest jab in the tournament and he knows it. He doesn't have to hit the other guy with strong hooks or even uppercuts. He can just keep jabbing and the more he works that left eye or the nose, one of two things will happen." George pointed to the fighter. "His eye, which is almost closed is finally going to shut all the way and then he won't be able to see his jab as he keeps going for the nose. Once he hits that nose, which is already starting to bleed, then it will start gushing blood. He won't be able to breath straight and when he can't see out of that left eye, he won't see the left hook that will put him on the canvas. He will be so out of breath that he won't get up. Of course, if the ref was as smart as I am h would call the fight already "

Liam watched carefully. George was right and it took just over a little thirty seconds for Quenton Hopkins to knock the other fighter out. Liam replied. "You were right." George smiled and winked at him. But that's what makes a good trainer, they see things that others can't and to anticipate what's going to happen just like in a chess match. Rarely do they need to say anything, they just know. The good ones always know…years of experience become their best teacher.

George Coghlan had seen it all… the fighter who is one punch from touching the canvas only to find that one lucky punch to knock the other guy out. He had seen too many times the fighter who had it won only to be drawn into a fighter's trap at the end and get taken out. More than once he had taken a fighter from the bottom to the top and made him a champion. And like all good trainers, they pass on their knowledge and build a fighter from the ground up, correcting their footwork, one step at a time. They teach them how to breath properly so they can conserve what they have in their tanks for the later rounds. Then you teach them how to throw a devastating punch that could end a fight before the audience can blink and how the real power in that punch comes from the legs when you have the proper footwork. You teach a fighter about strategy and what punch to throw and when. Just like there are building blocks in life, it's just as true when making a fighter, and with each instruction, Liam got one more building block.

When the fight was over, George drove him back to the Gym so they could get some work in and prepare for the fight. He didn't want to do too much, just some drills and shadow boxing so he could stay fresh. As they worked in one of the rings, Liam finally asked. "So how do I beat the guy I'm fighting tomorrow?"

George looked at him and then moved into position within one of the corners. "Big Daddy Johnson goes to the body more than any other fighter I've seen. He's going to rush you and push you into the corner or against the ropes and then come underneath and start punching away on your midsection. He won't throw a punch to your face until he feels you can't breathe anymore. "

"Oh...okay, how do I stop it? "

He had Liam get into a defensive stance and moved his arms more inside. "You're going to drop your hands and keep your arms inside your shoulders protecting your ribs. But while he's trying to get to the inside, you throw uppercuts... if he goes left, you go right with the uppercut and punch him in the nose and then you come underneath with the other hand. Then when he's going right, you hit him on the chin. You do that a few times and he will go down, but for this to work, you have to let him come to you. Let him put you in the corner. Let him keep trying to hit your midsection and then just him with the uppercuts."

"I thought getting put into the corner was a bad thing."

"Most of the time it is, but not if you're laying a trap or using it as a brace when you're trying to come inside with uppercuts...get it.

Liam nodded. " What if he goes for my head."

"Then you duck, come underneath with a good shot to the ribs and then come around with a good left or right hook depending on the direction he's coming from . I guarantee, you'll drop him and he won't get up, but the trick is to keep your hands inside your shoulders and come up from your legs with the uppercut. I know it will feel like an awkward position, but he leaves himself wide open to where you can hit him." They worked on it for the next hour. It was hard at first because a fighter's instincts is to keep their hands wide or straight ahead so they can jab and land good hooks. Liam got it down enough that George was satisfied, but only they would know for sure in a real fight,

The next night Liam was ready to fight Big Daddy Johnson. He wasn't nervous the like in the last fight. He felt more prepared. There were more people in the crowd that night. Liam was so focused on the fight and just ready to get started and everything leading up to it. He didn't hear the ref go over the rules. The only sound he was waiting for was the sound of the bell. As soon as the bell rang, the fight went as George predicted.

Johnson came out swinging and Liam let Johnson back him into the corner. He blocked most of the shots to the midsection. He was able to land uppercuts and the sound of the glove against Johnson's face sounded like an air gun...boom, boom...boom, boom...boom, boom. Three of them put

Johnson on the canvas, but he was able to get back up. However, Johnson was stunned and tried to shake it off. Liam did the exact same thing, he got backed into a corner, blocked the midsection shots, and threw a few more uppercuts to the chin and the nose...boom, boom...boom, boom...boom, boom.   The last one landed right on the nose and it's what put Big Daddy Johnson down. Liam knocked him out. Johnson made a small attempt to get up, but he was so woozy that he couldn't find his legs and fell to the canvas again. The last thing he heard was the ref reaching ten on the count. Johnson had to be helped by his trainer, if he had his wish, he would have just laid there on the canvas and passed out.

The announcer stated. " Wow, in thirty years of Boxing, I have never seen a fighter throw only upper cuts and knock someone out." The fight lasted a minute and twenty seconds. Liam didn't celebrate as much as he did with the last fight. He simply looked at George, stunned that he pretty much predicted how the fight would go. Whatever doubts he had about George knowing anything about boxing, they were gone now. Liam would never question George again...there was God and then there was his trainer and neither would ever be questioned.

After Liam got cleaned up and dressed he walked out of the locker room. Everybody was pretty much gone by now since his fight was the last of the evening. He was listening to music on his iPod and not paying attention as he turned the corner outside the locker room. He didn't see her and that's when they bumped into each other both losing their balance. She was the one who fell to the floor and as she got up, yelled. "What the fuck...look where you're going. " Liam was caught by surprise and felt guilty as he tried to help her up. " Sorry...my bad, I didn't see you."

"No shit. You should keep your head up, especially if your fighter."

Liam smiled. "Yeah, you should remember to do that. So what are you doing here...you're not here to clean the locker room?"

She got offended at his assumption. "No...I'm fighter too. I left something in there and just came back to get it."

"Oh...I didn't realize there were women fighters in the tournament."

She was offended even more and it showed in here tone. "Yeah, they allow women to box now? I mean, since men gave us right to vote... why not let us box too."

He gave her a sarcastic look. "Ha…that's not what I meant. I didn't think there were women fighters in this tournament."

She laughed. "Most people don't. We're not a big draw so our fights are early and we only have one division so they go quick and usually don't get noticed by the crowd. And you don't strike me as someone who cares about women fighters either."

"I don't care if women are boxers…I like women fighters."

"I call bullshit!"

"Honey, the neighborhood I'm from , every woman is a fighter…they have to be. So I have a great respect for women fighters."

She could tell that he was from a rougher part of Chicago. Probably one of the Irish neighborhoods. But she couldn't help but laugh at his comment. She replied. "Okay then, what's your name?"

"Liam Kelly."

She was a little stunned. "I've heard of you…yeah, you're the one that everybody was talking about tonight. The one who knocked out his opponent using only upper cuts within a minute of the first round."

"I only did what my trainer told me to do…it happened to work."

"I'll say. You're starting to get famous around here...pretty soon, people will be asking for your autograph and you'll probably expect me to sleep with you just because you're famous."

Liam smiled. "I'm just here to fight, not get my balls busted by a woman who thinks that I'm some asshole who can't stand women being equal." She gave a dirty look. He asked. "What's your name?"

"Molly Jansen"

"Good name. Are you still in the tournament."

Molly smiled. "Absolutely. Made it to the championship...I fight in a couple of days."

"Congrats. Maybe I will come and see you fight."

"Don't you have to fight two days from now... you probably shouldn't miss it. "

Liam laughed. " I don't plan on it, but I can do both. It's called multitasking."

"I don't know any man who can do that. But, I wouldn't hate it if you were there. Having another fighter cheer for me is a good thing."

"Well, Molly Jansen, I will see you then"

"Or you can buy me a cup of coffee... I know you were getting around to it eventually, after having looked at me so many times through the window at my gym...figured I would just speed that up."

Liam was surprised. "You saw me."

"Yeah...you're hard not to notice, so how about that cup of coffee."

He smiled at her. "Why not...better than staring through a window anyway."

She smiled at him and then they left together. She thought he was cute. He was intrigued by her because she was a fighter, but there was something else. Something brought them together, maybe it was a fate, but somehow he knew that she would be a friend, a lover, and that their connection could last a lifetime.

Molly and Liam ended up at a Diner in the neighborhood. It turned out they didn't live that far from each other. Liam lived in the predominately Irish neighborhood better known as the Bridgeport neighborhood. Molly lived just outside of it, but they went to a lot of the same places around the area. Their gyms were not that far from each other as well. Both of them at been to the Diner before and were somewhat regulars there. It was called, Paddy's and had been in the same family for three generations. Molly usually liked to get a to-go cup of coffee and Danish on her way to work. It always seemed better than Starbucks.

They grabbed a booth towards the back. As the waitress poured them each a cup of coffee, the owner of the place came by the table, mainly to speak with Liam. He was excited to see the lad. "Liam Kelly, you don't know how excited we've all been to see you on TV in the big tournament."

He smiled. "Thanks Malcolm, honestly, I didn't think anybody knew about it. "

"You forget this is a small world, especially if you fight, word gets around. Why didn't you say anything?"

"I just started training a couple of months ago. Wasn't going to make a big deal of it until I had my first fight."

"You're a big deal now…everybody around here has seen you fight. And I think you make a better boxer than a Hockey player."

Liam didn't know how to respond to that as he was still a little bitter about his hockey career ending. He changed the subject. " You know Molly, right?"

"Of course…it's good to see you in here at night and not just in the morning." She thanked him for the compliment. Liam responded. "She's a fighter too and is fighting for the Women's Division Championship."

Malcolm smiled. "Congratulations, and I hope you win, but don't let them mess up your face, you're far too pretty for that." The comment was a little misogynist, but she was the kind of girl who was never bothered by things like that. She had been around it, all of her life and she always had to take a lot of shit from men for being too pretty especially since she became a boxer. As far as she was concerned, she did her talking in the ring and the more she won, the more she proved everybody wrong. But it was still nice to get a compliment Malcolm left them to their coffee.

Molly said. "I told you, you were getting famous...your reputation precedes you."

Liam laughed. "I don't know about that, it's a small neighborhood and I think everybody gets bored easily...it's easy to entertain them even as an amateur boxer."

"Don't sell yourself short. Maybe they just need someone to believe in when there's not a lot of heroes around."

"I'm not any kind of hero...just another bum from the neighborhood."

"Why did you start fighting?"

"Because some old guy convinced me that my hockey career was over."

Molly gave him a strange look. "From what I understand that just happened recently."

"Two months ago."

"And you never thought about boxing before."

"Only fights I had ever been in were on the ice or fighting some guy from around here who disrespected my family or try to bully me."

"You most boxers have been doing it since they were teenagers and that's how they get their skills, you seem like a natural."

Liam smiled. "I guess I am…I've always been good at it. What about you? How did you get into fighting… you seem too smart to have to do it."

"I don't know if I have to do it, but I like boxing."

"I mean, you went to college, right."

"Yes, I did, graduate with a business degree, but even smart people can box."

"Sure, but I know why most guys get into it… they are not smart enough to do anything else that can make a big payday unless its crime. What made you really get into it."

Molly took a sip of coffee and then sat back in her chair. "A couple of years ago, I was at a party and two guys took advantage of me. I was drunk and they, how do I say it…"

Liam had a look of concern. "You mean, they raped you?"

She paused and her eyes started to well up. "Yeah...they raped me. I didn't have the strength to fend them off. I tried, but they pinned me down. The rest was a blur. I put myself out my mind to just to get through it."

"I'm sorry that happened to you...really, nobody should have to go through that. Guys who do that in my neighborhood usually end up in a ditch with their ball cut off.

Molly smiled. "Thank you. I made a decision after it happened that I would never be a victim again. I would know how to fight back so I started learning how."

"Why boxing...why not MMA or kickboxing."

"They're good sports, but there's something eloquent about boxing... something poetic...standing there toe to toe with someone and using nothing but your fists. Being able to take a punch and then give one right back. It's simple, it's brutal, and you stand face to face, looking your enemy in the eye, no tricks, just punch after punch until one of you goes down. There's something beautiful about it!"

Liam smiled. "Damn, I was just going to say it's a lot more fun to hit someone. But I like what you said better." They both laughed. Molly responded with a question. "Why do you want to be a boxer and don't say it's because you just want to fight...now that you're doing it, why do you want to keep doing it, or have you not thought about it."

"Actually, I was thinking about it last night. Truth is, I don't mind fighting, never have. But I know that I don't want to be a typical guy from the neighborhood, going nowhere. Guy's like that end up in jail or dead. I want to fight enough to where I don't have to fight anymore and make enough money that I don't have to worry about anything anymore."

"I don't know if it works that way with money, but I understand wanting to be better than the typical guy from around here. Boxing can be a way out, but don't you want to be a champion one day?"

"Liam smiled. "Of course, who wouldn't want to be a champion! But I want to be more than that... I want to be a legend, I think that's better."

Molly smiled. "A legend uh, well, I would say that you're on your way." She finished her cup of coffee. "I should probably get home, but don't think for a moment that just because you bought me a cup of coffee and have a nice smile, that I'm going to sleep with you."

He was taken back by the comment, but liked her feistiness. He playfully replied.

"What if I bought you dinner and had a nice smile…what would happen then?"

"You're cute Liam Kelly and maybe I will let you buy me dinner, but for now."

"For now, I should at least be a gentleman and walk you home."

She smiled. There was an attraction. She couldn't deny that. He thought she was stunning and being a boxer just made her even sexier. Liam never considered that to be a turn on. But here they were, attracted to one another and wondering what next. She found the answer the next morning as she got up early from Liam's bed and stared out his bedroom window at the snow beginning to fall against a gray Chicago sky . Some of the best things that happen to us are not planned…they are accidents waiting to happen.

ROUND 8

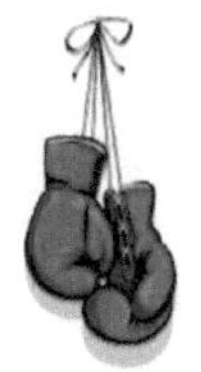

The Tournament was winding down. Most weight divisions were down to just four boxers. All except the Womens Division. There championship fight was tonight. Liam got to the ballroom early. He didn't want to miss the women's championship fight. It was two rounds in and Molly was doing good . She had already scored a knockdown and was ahead on points. George found him in the stands. He was a little miffed. Liam was late and needed to be getting ready for his own fight. He yelled. "Liam what the hell are you doing...did you forget that you had a fight tonight?"

Liam was stunned. He had lost track of time. "Sorry, I wanted to see this fight."

"What...the women's round! You have more important things to do."

"I met one of them last night. "

"Geez...let me guess, she was cute, and if you root for her, then you have a good chance to sleep with her. "

Liam gave him a dirty look. "It's not like that."

"Save it. I'm a guy too. I know how it works, but if you want my advice...."

Liam cut him off. "You're going to tell me that women weaken legs."

"Actually, no...that's not true at all! They fuck with your head...not your legs."

"Really!"

"Yeah, and clearly you've never been married. What I was going to say was...win the tournament and impress her that way since she's a boxer. But to do that then you have to get ready."

Liam smiled. "And I guess, you're going to tell me how to win."

For fuck's sake, haven't you learned anything yet...listen to me and you will definitely win."

They got to the locker room. Liam had to get ready fast. Taping him up was even faster. As they were waiting to walk out to the ring, George spoke up. "Alright, kid...here's how you're going to beat Fast Eddie Jackson.

He's faster than you are. Won't lie to you, but that doesn't mean you can't beat him.   He relies mostly on his jab, and he is faster than anyone I have seen in a long time. But don't worry about that. You can beat it. He will try and keep his distance so he can land more and more jabs. You're going to keep your head down more than usual and come underneath. Every time he throws that left jab...you come underneath and put a left uppercut in his ribs. Just like before, keep breaking him down until he can't breath and then you will be able to throw hooks and straight shots as he starts protecting his ribs more. That's how you knock him out. But, it's not going to happen in the first round. You will have to take your time and wear him down."

Liam nodded. "I will have to stay lower than I normally do...so almost bend down."

"Exactly, plus it will you give you more power from your legs when you land those upper cuts. What have I been saying...power comes from your legs! "

Liam smiled. "I haven't forgotten."

"Good...now, I want you to do something that most trainers would not recommend...let him hit you a couple of times and when you throw your first punch...miss it on purpose."

Liam look confused. George responded. "I know, it sounds like the wrong advice, but I want this guy to start feeling too confident with those jabs. Let him hit you couple of times…miss your first punch, and then he will think you can't fight. He'll get over confident and won't worry about technique as much. "That's when you have him. Over confidence is the worst thing that can happen to a fighter…he forgets how to fight."

They walked to the ring. The crowd was bigger than it had been over the last few days and their cheers made up for the lack of walk out music. As they met in the middle of the ring while the referee was going over the rules, Eddie Jackson didn't take his eyes of Liam. He didn't say much except, "first round mother fucker, " just to let Liam know that he wouldn't make it out of the first round. His taunts didn't phase Liam at all. By this point, he had learned not to say anything and let his fists do the talking.

The fight started. Liam did exactly what his trainer told him to do. He let Jackson hit him a couple of times with that left jab. Liam thought to himself, he was fast, but stuck to the plan, he got hit a few times and then wildly threw a left hook and missed. It was embarrassing and it felt awkward to do that, but it seemed to work. Eddie Jackson had this confident smile like he had already won the fight. Liam lowered is head a little more as Jackson kept throwing that left jab. There was a smooth rhythm to it...jab, jab...jab, jab...then he would throw a right hook. Some shots were landing, but Liam was getting out of the way of most of them. Finally, as a left jab came towards Liam's head, he slipped underneath and put all his power into a left uppercut and crashed it into Jackson's ribs. Eddie cringed. One of his ribs was cracked. Liam was also able to land a right hook on top of that.   Jackson almost went down, but jabbed some more, landing a few headshots and creating some distance. Liam spent most of the first round chasing him and never really landed any good punches. But he had a cut below his eye and it was something to be concerned about.

As Liam sat down in his corner, he said. "He's too fast, I can't catch him. "

George worked on the cut below his eye. "I told you he was faster, but you can beat him. And you're going to have to do it fast. If he hits you on this cut a few more times then it will be a blood bath that I can't stop and they will call the fight."

"I thought this was part of your plan."

George shrugged. "Didn't think he would cut you with his jabs, but nothing to be concerned about...you still have this."

"Then what do I do...rush him and just beat him like it's a street fight."

"It's too early for that. Don't chase him...make him come to you, some where near the ropes or a corner. When he throws that left jab, get down even lower and grab with your hands and arms and spin him around where his back is against the corner or ropes and he can't go anywhere. Put a couple of shots into his ribs ad then an uppercut on his chin. If he tries to move block him with the other arm and keep him there and keep landing body shots until he can barely stand. Now don't let him hold you or this isn't going to work. When you see your chance, come around with that left and knock him out. One good shot is all it takes."
The bell rang for the second round. Liam met him in the center of the ring and then started to back up towards a corner while jabs came his way. Eddie Jackson fell for it. He came at Liam, but still had some distance. Jab, jab...jab, jab! Most of them missed, but Eddie kept throwing them hoping some would land. Liam lowered his body and with his right hand and arm, grabbed Jackson by the waist and spun him around as he was throwing

another jab. He got turned around and pushed him up against the red corner guard.

Jackson didn't know what happened and before he could throw a punch, Liam jammed his left into Jackson's cracked ribs and a right uppercut into the other side. Jackson was hurt, he couldn't hid the look on his face from the pain,   Liam landed an uppercut to Jackson's chin. He started to go down and caught himself on the ropes. Liam had his moment. As Jackson was coming back up, Liam crashed a left hook into his face. It rocked him so hard that his feet came out from underneath him and he fell backwards almost out of the bottom of the ring. He had to grab the ropes just to keep himself in the ring.

Liam was directed to one of the corners. By the time the ref got over to the man on the canvas, he took one look at Eddie Jackson and didn't even administer the ten count. Jackson passed out as he tried to get up. The ref waved his hands and the fight was over. The second round happened so fast that most people didn't even see the left hook that knocked Jackson out. One of the spectators on the front row, yelled out. "Did you see that phantom punch...just like Ali."

Liam jumped up in celebration and George came inside the ring and hugged him. He said. Didn't I tell you that would work."

Liam was amazed…he had never done that move before. His adrenaline was flowing so much that he was talking shit. He said. "Bring me the next guy and I will do it again. Fuck me, I love that move. " George just laughed. As Liam looked around the crowd, he spotted Molly Jansen. She was sitting towards the back in the first set of rows. She was wearing gym clothes and holding a small size belt. Molly clapped for Liam, but he pointed at her and clapped for her with his gloves still on, congratulating her on winning the women's division.

George let him have his moment. He deserved it, but he knew that it would be short lived. Before the fight started he found out whom Liam would be fighting if he won the semi finals. It was pretty much a forgone conclusion because everybody had been saying that this guy would be in the finals and would probably win it all. He was menacing and had beaten all of opponents in the first round. Even now, despite how well Liam had done in the tournament, he was a huge underdog. He would have to fight the man they called the Bazooka…Kenny, "the

Bazooka" Allen and it wasn't going to be easy like the last three

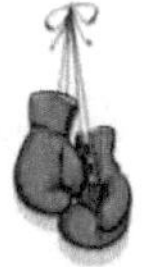

   Liam finished cleaning up and he only had one thought on his mind. The Championship. He had made it to the final round. Honestly, he couldn't believe it. Yes, he knew how to fight, but that was street fighting. Boxing was all together something different. And after nearly two months of training, he still felt that he didn't know anything. Most of what he was doing was the blind instinct of just throwing punches like he had done hundreds of times on the streets in his neighborhood or being the goon for any hockey team he had ever been on. He didn't go out and party like most people would. He went home, but he couldn't sleep. He was too excited, to pumped up because he was in the champion and won three boxing matches. He knew that his trainer would tell him to try and sleep, but all he seemed to do was stare at the ceiling. So Liam went running. He ran through his neighborhood and to his surprise, people were congratulating him.

He stopped by Murphy's Pub and when he walked in he got a standing ovation. That had never happened to him before. He sat down at the bar and Vic poured him a Guinness. He was surprised at how excited seemed to be over his victory. He still didn't think it was that big of a deal.

He said to Vic after taking a sip of Guinness "Why is everybody so excited. It's just an amateur tournament."

" Since you don't know a whole lot of boxing, let me educate you. It's the All Chicago Boxing Tournament... it's a big deal here in Chicago, especially now because an Irishman hasn't won it since 1959."

"Really!"

"Oh yeah...usually some black guy wins it. To make it this far, you've made everybody proud. You're like a hero or something. You win the whole damn thing and you will be a legend round here."

"Liam smiled. He had never thought about that. But then again, even he couldn't remember the last local hero from the neighborhood. If there were any, it was way before his time. He finished his Guinness and as he walked out, everybody clapped for him. There were murmurs from the crowd, telling him good luck. One old guy even said. " You beat that nigger." Liam didn't appreciate the comment and gave the man a dirty look. Unfortunately, sometimes Irishmen could be just as racist as southern rednecks that longed for the good ole days of segregation. But Liam was touched by the outpour of congratulations. It was inspiring and he wanted to make everybody proud. Up until this point he was only fighting for himself, but now, in no small way, he was fighting for those who didn't seem to have any hope all. To those in his neighborhood, he had a better chance of bringing hope to their lives than the black senator running for president.

Later that evening, George grabbed a bite to eat and had a few drinks at The King's Club. It was an old fashioned Private Club in Chicago for men only, not a strip joint, but the kind of social club that men could escape to and get away from wives, children, and any kind of responsibility. Men didn't have to put on a façade...they could be the worst of themselves and leave morality at the door. Normally, women weren't allowed unless they were a working girl. But every once in a while, one with enough balls could get past the doorman. Pricilla was that kind of women. Mostly because she could survive in a man's world and could always stand up to her husband who had been a member. She found George sitting at the bar with a glass of twenty-five year McCallan Scotch.

He should have been surprised to see her, but he knew her stubbornness could get her through any door in this town She sat down and ordered the same thing as George . At first the bartender gave her a funny look because she was a woman, but she gave him a dirty look right back. He poured her a drink and then she said to George.

"Your boy looked good out there tonight... I can see why you started training him. He definitely has the goods."

"Told you."

"She laughed. "You haven't always been right."

"Most of the time I am and sometimes I did it just for the money."

"We all sell out a little bit...it's natural."

"So what are you doing here, you know my ritual after my fighter wins."

"Yes, I know you like to be left alone, When Frank was still alive, you two would retreat here after a big fight like you were kids hanging out in your personal clubhouse where girls aren't allowed."

George smiled. "You make it sound like a bad thing."

"I'm here about business…I'm assuming your plan was to take the kid pro and let him rise through the ranks until he get's a title shot."

"Something like that and I know, I was supposed to retire. That's what you're going to say, right!"

"Nobody who knows you, actually thought you would retire. You will always find another fighter to train. It's what you do and you can never get away from what your supposed to do."

"How can you help."

"I can get you a professional fight and the purse would be forty grand."

George looked at her with disbelief. "A fight with who?"

"Davis Dean… the guy he was supposed to fight, broke his hand and it won' be healed in time."

"How long?"

"Fight is in six weeks."

George sighed. "That's not a whole lot of time to get ready especially if Liam takes a good beating in the next match."

"I know, but after watching him, I think he can beat Davis Dean and I don't want to cancel this fight because we can't find someone. "

George paused for a moment. "Isn't he ranked like number ten?"

"He actually fell to 15th.

"I don't know, I wanted something a little easier for his professional debut."

"Dean is not the fighter he used to be. You honestly think your boy can't win, this would be a good fight for him and beating Dean would do wonders for his confidence.

"I want him to be ready…to be completely ready for a professional boxer who has more experience."

She smiled. "I understand that, but you can't hold him back either…you have to see what he can really do out there…beyond this tournament."

"Look Pricilla, this is my last shot at training a potential champion…I want to do it right."

"So this is really about you and learning from your mistakes. It's not about your fighter!"

George gave her a dirty look. "Of course it's about him, but it's also learning from my experience. When he gets a title shot, I want him to be ready for it so he can win and have the experience to hold on to it. That's all, but if I rush him and he loses a fight, he may never come back from it."

She smiled. "I understand that, but don't let your ego hold him back. If there's one thing that my husband taught me, fighters have to be challenged or they can't be good fighters."

He laughed. "That's what I taught your husband when he was first starting out."

"I know, but sometimes we need to be reminded of our own lessons."

"Touche, my dear."

Pricilla patted him on the back. "I'm offering you a fight, you let me know if you want it."

"Can I make that decision after the tournament championship?"

"You have a few days to make up your mind, but let your fighter decide too. This his career, remember that."

"Why do I feel like you're my mother?"

"Sometimes we have to be...men always think they know everything. And then we come along and make sure you know the right answer."

George didn't like to here that, but he couldn't argue with her logic. It reminded him of his wife and she was usually right, at least most of the time. Pricilla finished her scotch and left. George should have been happy, Liam had his first professional fight booked, but in his mind, it wasn't time to celebrate. He didn't know how Liam would fair against his next opponent... the outcome of that would really determine whether he should take the next fight. It was supposed to be easy to say yes to your first professional fight, but George could be like an overprotective parent at times with his fighters. At the end of the day, it was about protecting him. And he still hadn't come up with a strategy for beating Kenny Allen yet. Right now, there didn't seem to be a way to beat him...he looked invincible. But that was a problem for tomorrow. Tonight he quietly celebrated the fact that his fighter had made it this far and in a few days he would be fighting in the tournament championship within the heavyweight division. He was proud even if he didn't show it.

The championship fight was a few days away. Everything about it seemed surreal. A few months ago, he was just a minor league hockey player and now on his way to becoming a professional boxer. He tried to relax. He had been told to take it easy and let his bruises heal, but sitting still and relaxing was never easy for him. Molly had spent the last couple of nights at his place. They ordered take out and spent most of the time in bed. She had propped her championship belt up at the foot of Liam's bed so she could marvel at her accomplishment. It was definitely worth bragging about even if it was just an amateur tournament.

As they sat in bed, Molly commented. "I think this just may be the best belt, I've ever owned. I may not be able to wear it with anything practical, but still...it's the best belt in my collection."

Liam laughed. "It is a nice belt. I have to admit."

"You know what will make it look better...your championship belt next to mine."

"You're absolutely right, but you have to wait a few days."

"Are you nervous?"

"About the fight...nah...it's just another fight."

Molly gave him a strange look. "Really, you have seen the guy you're fighting, right...I mean he looks ferocious."

"That's what everybody keeps saying, but I've fought tough guys before and won. I won't be afraid of this guy."

"I don't want you to be afraid, but I don't want you to take this fight too lightly."

Liam was surprised. "You think I am?"

"Honestly, I can't tell. All I know is you can get seriously hurt by this guy and I don't want to see that."

Liam kissed her. "I completely understand and your concern is nice, but if I am too nervous then I won't fight good and that's what I am mostly worried about. Win or lose, I won't make it easy for him."

"Just want to make sure you have the right frame of mind because I want you to win...you're too good not to win this thing. And I don't want to be a distraction."

He kissed her again. "You're not a distraction....not at all. I actually feel more at peace right now than I have in a long time."

Molly smiled. "Good."

"But seriously, you have to work on your pep talks. That was terrible. He said sarcastically

She was about to respond and then all of sudden there was a knock at the door. Liam got up to answer and when he opened the door that peaceful feeling turned to shock. It was his father, smiling as if nothing had ever happened between them. Liam responded. "What the fuck do want?"

His father replied. "What...I can't catch up with my son."

"How do you know where I live?"

"It's a small neighborhood, it's not hard to find someone. Besides, I saw the news, you're fighting for the championship in the All Chicago Boxing Tournament, I just wanted to tell you, congratulations... I'm proud of you som" Before Liam could reply, Molly asked. "Who is it?"

"It's my father unfortunately."

"Well invite him in, I want to meet him." His father replied. "Yeah, why don't you invite me in so I can meet your girlfriend or is she your wife?" Reluctantly he let his father into the apartment and replied. "I'm not married."

Molly introduced herself and chatted with the old man for a little bit, trying to get to know him..trying to get a sense of what kind of man he was. He did the same with her, but with him it was more about sizing her up and seeing how gullible she might be. He always had an angle. He was only sincere when he needed something. After the small , his father finally asked.

"So Liam, how are you feeling...ready to fight?"

"Why do you want to know?"

"I'm just concerned. I want my son to win and if you need any help, I'm here. I may not have been there for you as a kid, but I'm here now."

Liam gave him a strange look. "Really, I call bullshit on that."

"Look, I know you have no reason to trust me, but I'm being serious, just looking out for you so you can win."

"What are the odds on me?"

"What are you talking about?"

"The odds... am I a three to one underdog... five to one....ten to one. I think you're looking to put some action on the fight and you're pumping me for information."

"I heard the odds were eight to one against you, but I'm not betting on the fight."

"Bullshit...that's exactly what you're doing. You're a gambling junkie, you can't help it."

His father laughed. "Wow, you really don't know me."

"No, because you walked out on me and my mother ten years ago and were never really around before that anyway. And when you were there, all you did was cause trouble... making our lives worset than they should have been. "

"That's not fair...there's more to it than that and your mother was no saint."

Liam shot him a dirty look. "You don't talk about her. What's not fair is the heroin addiction that you gave her because you wanted to test out the product you were selling." His father gave him a funny look. Liam responded. "Yeah, I know about that. She never could shake it and eventually, it killed her. That's on you."

His father tried to say something, but he was cut off. Molly had a horrified look on her face as if what she was hearing could only be exaggerated. But after spending a few minutes in the same room as Liam's father and seeing how shady he really was, it was easier to believe the truth. Liam simply said to his father after cutting him off. "Get the fuck out of here. I can't ban you from the city or even this neighborhood, but you stay out of my life."

His father left. Molly was shocked. Maybe she shouldn't have been, it's not like she really knew a whole lot about Liam and his past. But it was still shocking to see what had just happended. She said, "I'm sorry you had to deal with that."

He replied. "It's not your fault. I'm sorry you had to see that."

"You haven't seen him in ten years?"

"Yeah, when he walked out and never came home one night with all the money we had at the time. I was fifteen. He was dealing heroin at the time… said he was trying to unload the product to a friend, but he would cook it down to make more so he could increase his profits. He would also test it out on him and my mother. She got hooked on it and kept the habit for the next couple of years until she finally OD'ed. Never heard from him again until a few days ago. To be honest, I thought he was dead, but I guess that was just wishful thinking."

Molly held him and then she kissed him. "Nobody should have to go through it."

"No, but Irish stories usually don't have a happy ending. I guess that's why Irish Songs always sound bitter, we like to celebrate our misery."

"Or it's a good excuse to be a fighter…you get to punch out all of your hate in the ring."

Liam smiled. "I would agree with that."

ROUND 9

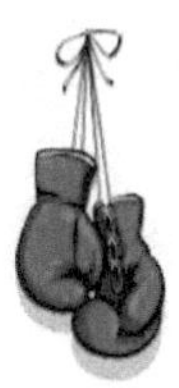

It was in the afternoon when Liam finally made it to the Holy Trinity gym for a light workout and to get a rub down. But also, he was to go over strategy on how to beat Kenn y Allen. George was watching film of his last three fights. There wasn't much to work with since Allen had knocked out his opponents out in the first round. The fights never lasted long enough to really get a sense of how Allen fought and what kind of style he had. All George really knew is that he was a brawler, used to knocking guys out with one punch. Fighters like that always seemed talented, but they could get exposed easily if they had to fight ten or twelve rounds. Brawling couldn't take the place of technique and good fight strategy.

As Liam and George started watching the videos of Allen' last fights, George commented. "I'll be honest…this is going to be a tough fight…he can hit hard and take you out with one punch."

"I've known guys like that."

"This isn't some guy from your neighborhood. This guy is a wrecking ball and from what I can tell, he just wails on you until he gets that one big punch to take you out. And worse, his swings are solid. They're not wild and land with accuracy uncommon with a big brawler."

Liam replied. "You act like he doesn't have a weakness."

"I'm not saying that, just want you to be aware that this is going to be tough and you're going to have to stick to a strategy that it will take the full fight. You are fighting eight rounds this time and honestly it will take eight rounds to beat him. Don't be surprised if it's decided by the judges."

"I don't know if I can go the distance, I mean I'm in shape and all, but eight rounds of boxing will be tough."

Yes it will, but it's also what you have going for you. He hasn't gone that far in a fight as well, which means you will have to wear him down. He hits harder, he's probably faster than you are, but he probably doesn't have the stamina that you do."

"So he's my Apollo Creed."

"More like your Clubber Lang."

Liam laughed. George responded. "Everybody knows Ali's Rope-A-Dope and I doubt it would really work in an a eight round fight. You can only really get that once before they know you're secret.

"So what do we do?"

"Quick jabs and go to the body. One thing I have noticed is his big punches are really just two punch combos...one quick jab and then a fading hook because he's usually punching down. I think he telegraphs it, which means it will be easier to move right or left and come underneath it. And that's when you go to the body. You will have to work your punches into his ribs for a few a few rounds to make it harder for him to breath and wear him down."

"Always to the body, right!"

"That's usually the rule. Hitting the face is flashy and looks good on TV, but you win fights by going to the body. Especially when your opponent is taller. The fact that Allen is two inches taller than you will be a good advantage for you...it will be easier to get underneath, but you will have to watch out for those big punches. One punch can put you down and that's the match. The other thing I want you to do is keep your distance until you can work your way underneath. Dance with him and jab."

"I don't know if my footwork is good enough."

"Maybe not, but you can't stand toe- to-toe with this guy. So dance with him...use the entire ring."

There was doubt in Liam's voice. "Do you think he's the better fighter?"

George paused for a moment. "Probably, but you can beat him...I believe you can win because I think you have more heart than he does. This guy knows he can win and his overconfidence is his weakness. You're not sure if you can win, but you won't back down. You have the courage to get in that ring. That means you have more heart and I'll take that any day of the week when comes to winning the fight."

Liam smiled. "What else do I need to know?"

"The rest we will have to figure round by round just in case he changes his style. Now let's go work on moving around his combo punches. " The fighter and the trainer went to one of the rings and starting working on getting out of the way of being punched. They worked on Liam's dance moves as silly as it sounded . They prepared the best they could for the upcoming battle for which victory was far from certain.

When they were done, Liam left and went home to get some rest. George went into the office and found Paul. He asked. "Did you get what I needed?"

"I took care of it. Your stuff will be here tomorrow and Bill will be here too as your cut man.

"Thank You."

"I must say, he looked really good in the tournament."

George tried to smile. "He's looking good so far. Let's see what happens Saturday."

"Are you saying that because you don't want to admit I was right to put him in the tournament?"

"He's done good, better than expected, but the guy he's fighting..."

Paul cut him off. "I know, he's a wrecking machine, but you know your boy can win, don't you. "

"He can, but can he survive the battle he's about to go through. It will be the ultimate test on whether he can be a professional fighteror not. I just don't know if he's ready for that yet."

"You know, you worry too much."

George smiled. "I know, but it's my job to worry so my fighter doesn't have to."

"And you love it."

George smiled and nodded in agreement as he left the office.

It was customary to have a press conference before each Championship Match in the All Chicago Boxing Tournament. It was a chance for the media to get to know the future champion and those who were soon to become professional boxers. It was also a chance for the fighters to get used to talking to the media and to go through a real press conference, the kind that would happen before big fights. It was like a movie star walking a Red Carpet for the first time. Liam was not that excited. He just wanted to fight and didn't see what a press conference had to do with that. But he hadn't learned how to really sell a fight, yet...there was an art to it. Part of the job was getting people excited about the fight and not every fighter could be like Muhammad Ali where it was just natural.

The Chicago tournament was not really national news so it was just local media there except for a couple of national reporters. They were there because of George Coghlan. He was one of the most famous trainers in the last thirty years and anytime he trained a boxer, it was national sports news. George knew why they were there and even though he didn't want his past overshadowing Liam's night, he also knew that it was good exposure, a chance to shed some of that national spotlight on up-and-coming boxer that he hoped in a few years would get a title shot.

Everybody got seated. George leaned over and said to Liam. "Just so you know this is when the fight starts... you sell it, then you fight." Both fighters were at a loss at what to do. The tournament director started off the press conference by announcing the fighters and giving their stats. Liam Kelly, 6'3" and weighing in at 225 pounds. Kenny "The Bazooka" Allen, 6'5" and weighing in at 240 pounds. He opened the floor to questions. The first one went to Kenny Allen. The reporter asked. "You haven't had to go past the first round so far in the tournament, how are you prepared if this goes the full fight." Allen didn't say much. "The white boy is just another chump, I'll knock him out in the first round just like the others." The same reporter asked Liam. "Do you have a response to that?"

Liam replied. "Sure, maybe he's just saying that because he can't count higher than one." Everybody laughed. Liam understood that these press conferences were for the most part about talking trash and creating an animosity between the fighters. He used the opportunity to get some figurative jabs in. Allen wasn't amused and yelled out. "Motherfucker, I'll come over there right now and knock you out." Liam stood up and yelled. "Come over here and do it...let's start this thing now." Allen stood up and tried to go after him as Liam was trying to throw a punch . The other folks at the table had to get in between them to stop a fight from breaking out. When everything was settled down, a reporter from ESPN asked George. "Mr. Coghlan, you essentially retired after the Tommy Franks debacle in his Championship fight over a year ago, why are you training another boxer?"

George answered. "I was never really retired, just took some time off until I found a new project."

The reporter asked. "It doesn't have anything to do with the fact that you were sued by ACM Management and blacklisted by them from getting any championship fights or work with any of their contenders and that's why you haven't trained anybody of significance in a year?" Liam was taken back; he had never heard this before. Was his trainer tainted. That's all he could think about now.

George replied. "I think you have been misinformed. I am not blacklisted from anything and even though ACM and I parted ways under bad circumstances, I can train who I want and get them a fight with whom I want. But the thing to remember is I choose who I train and I chose Liam Kelly because of his potential. And in my book, he is already a champion and that's all I am going to say. This is about Liam and the fight tomorrow."

The press conference went on a little while longer with the usual bullshit questions about each fighter's style and what they hoped to achieve. They were the kind of uninteresting things that made people change the channel. But the press conference did end with some fireworks. As it was wrappingup, Kenny Allen tried to get the last world and irritate Liam and made sure everybody could hear what he was sure would be and explosive sound bite. He said. "Hey white boy, tell your mother she gets the privilege of sucking the Champ's dick tomorrow night...I promise, I'll be gentle."

He shouldn't have let it bother him, he knew the insult didn't mean anything, just strategy to get him off his game before the big fight, but this was about his mother. That was going to far and any man who crossed the line insulting someone's mother, deserved to be punished. It was a weakness for sure, but he didn't care. Liam jumped out of his chair and charged Allen. He got one unch in and Allen pushed him towards the conference table, trying to get in some punches of his own before everybody broke up the fight. It didn't work out that way. Between the people trying to break it up and Allen pinning Liam down on the conference table, two of Liam's fingers got broken. The fighters got pulled apart and sent out of the room in separate directions. The press got plenty of video and pictures. By the morning and with the help of the internet, the buzz surrounding this fight would spread like a wildfire throughout Chicago and surround areas. By the morning, it was the main event in the city and the local sports teams would garnish such popularity. The press conference worked even if it didn't go according to plan.

George checked Liam's fingers. "They're broken, we will have to tape them together before we tape you for the fight. You will have to let them swell up right before the fight so you don't feel anything during the match or its going to hurt like hell and you won't be able to punch as effective."

"Sorry about the fingers."

"No big deal...we can fix it and you did well during the conference... you sold the fight. After this hits the net and local news,everybody will want to see it so good job. You just might be a natural at this part of boxing."

"So why didn't you tel tell me about ACM and being blacklisted."

George chuckled. "Because it's not that important. I'm not blacklisted and it won't affect you being able to get fights."

"Don't get me wrong, I trust you, but at the same time..."

George cut him off. " I get it, if I'm damaged goods then am I really the best option for you as a trainer."

"Yeah, something like that."

"It's a valid point, this is not the time to think about it. You have a fight tomorrow and the guy who you just seriously pissed off will tryi to kill you in the ring. Your mind needs to be focused on that and how to win tomorrow. So for the rest of the day... you relax and try to get as much rest as possible." Liam didn't say anything...there wasn't anything more for

him than tomorrow night. It was the biggest
fight of his life...win or lose!

        Liam was up early. Tonight he would
fight and it wasn't just any fight. He got some
sleep last night after making love to Molly.
But it wasn't a full night's sleep and
surprisingly, he wasn't tired. He was at peace.
Most fighters would be nervous. He got up
and made some coffee. Molly was still asleep.
He had one cup and then did something he
hadn't done in a long time...he went to
morning mass at St. Thomas' Catholic
Church. As he walked through the doors
people would shake his hand and tell him
good luck. He hadn't quite grasped how big of
a deal this was in his neighborhood. Yeah Vic
told him it was, but that was just one man's
opinion and Vic could be full of shit
sometimes. It started to sink in when more
and more people came up to him to tell him
good luck. After mass was done, even Father
Joseph made a point to wish him the best and

that he would say a blessing for him before the fight.

The day went by fast and that was fine with Liam, he just wanted to get to it. Let the fight begin. George had told him to load up on carbs in the morning...pancakes, eggs, and sausage. He and Molly went to the diner that morning and got a huge breakfast. The rest of the day he ate fruit and stayed hydrated. He didn't know where he and Molly were at this point. Were they dating or just messing around. Either way, he was glad to have her there with him. His fight was at nine pm. The Cruiserweight and Light Heavyweight championship were the two fights before him. Even though the Heavyweight division was not as popular in boxing anymore, it was still the premier division in Chicago and it's championship fight always came last in the tournament. It was still the biggest draw. Liam got to the Aragon Ballroom early. It was busy, but not all the seats were filled when he arrived. Maybe it wasn't going to be as full as he thought. The capacity was five thousand seats and you could put an additional five hundred seats around a boxing ring when placed in the middle of the floor.

Liam went to the locker room while Molly went to find a seat. She didn't need to be a distraction. George smiled when he saw Liam. "Hey kid…are you ready."

Liam smiled back. "Let's fight."

"That's what I want to hear. Come here, I want to introduce you to our cut man for the evening, this is Bill Waters." Liam and Bill shook hands and Bill got a good look at his face, checking for imperfections that might be a problem during the fight as well as his other wounds to see if they had healed enough. He replied. "Not perfect, but I've seen worse. We should be fine tonight."

George said to Liam. "Bill and I go way back. He's the best cut man that I have ever worked with and he will keep any amount of blood from gushing so the ref doesn't call the fight before it's done. Also, I have something for you." George brought Liam over to the dressing table, there was a large box on it. Liam opened it and found a pair of new boxing gloves, green, white, and orange…the color of the Irish National Flag. There was also a new pair of shorts, mostly white, with green and orange trim. And the last thing in the box was a new robe, mostly green with orange and white trim. His name was on the back. Liam was surprised; he didn't think he had earned any of this yet. That's what he told George.

George replied. "Regardless of what happens tonight, you've earned it…you'r a professional fighter now and I thought your gear should reflect that as well as bare the colors of a Proud Irishman."

Liam didn't really have the words to properly thank his trainer. But they weren't needed...his look of gratitude said enough. It was time to get ready. Liam got dressed in his new shorts and they went perfectly with his white boxing shoes, that weren't really fancy, but were comfortable and that's all he needed for a fight. So they started taping his hands and making sure that his broken fingers sealing with enough tape that he could still punch. One of the refs and someone from his opponent's side were in there to make sure the tape job was proper. Finally the taped hands were marked with a sharpie marker to indicate that they checked out. Liam shadowboxed and got loose. It was getting closer to the first bell and finally it was time to put on his new Gloves.

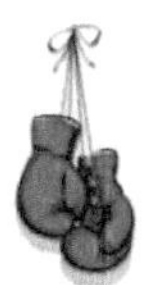

Vic was trying to get the big TV hooked up at Murphy's Pub and not having any luck. Some how the connections were off and all anybody saw was a blue screen. It was getting close to time for the fight to start and the small TV's there weren't going to cut it since the Pub was so crowded. One of the regulars finally asked Vic. "We don't have that much time, are you going to get that thing figured out?"

"Not if you keep bothering me," Vic replied.

"Well, you look like you don't know what you're doing."

Vic peered out from behind the TV. "If I give you a free beer, will you shut up and leave me alone."   "Yeah, that would make me shut up." The regular got his free beer and a few minutes later, Vic finally figured it out and got the TV working. They found the correct Comcast sports channel and they had a large screen to watch the fight, it everything they needed to make the evening a good one. Everybody in the pub cheered when they saw the Aragon Ballroom on the TV. It was about time for the fighters to start walking too the ring. . The ballroom was starting to fill up. It was getting close to capacity and from what Vic could tell, it looked as is if there were a lot of people from the neighborhood who somehow scored a ticket. He turned around and told the regulars who were sitting at the bar. "I told you we wouldn't miss Liam's fight.

No way in hell would I let that happen." They
all applauded for him.

The announcers were finishing their
pre-game coverage. They were a couple of
local Sports Casters, Chip Davis and Roger
Bennett, not necessarily experts in boxing,
but great announcers and they worked well
with one another. They had done play by play
for this tournament, the last few years. Chip
started giving a little background on the
fighters...

"The final fight of the evening is one of
the more interesting battles we've had in a
long time within this tournament. We have
two brawlers from similar neighborhoods in
the sense of how tough it is to survive there.
The advantage in this fight goes to Kenny "The
Bazooka" Allen, who is two inches taller and
twenty pounds heavier. He is from the
Southside of Chicago near from what used to
be Maxwell Street. He boxed in Golden Gloves
and has yet to face an opponent that he
couldn't knock out in the first few rounds. He
is sometimes referred to as a wrecking

machine and has certainly lived up to the name. He is favored to win, but has never faced anyone like his challenger, Liam Kelly. Liam is a former hockey player who was drafted by St. Louis at seventeen, but never made it to the NHL. Considered at one time to be a top defensive prospect, he has pretty much been what is called the goon on any team he's played because his fighting abilities. It seems only right that he would transition into boxing, but is relatively inexperienced. He has done well so far and appears to have some skill, but the biggest advantage he has is being trained by legendary trainer George Coghlan, who appears to have come out of retirement to train the young Kelly. Liam Kelly is an Irishman from the Bridgeport neighborhood and has gained a reputation as a brawler, but he has demonstrated some interesting techniques that have allowed him to easily the first three rounds of this tournament."

Roger chimed in. " And we saw that in what has become known as the uppercut fight, where he knocked the guy out using only upper cuts. With these two fighters, I think everybody should get ready for a battle. While both of these fighters have won their previous matches in in two rounds or less, I'm predicting that this fight will go the full eight rounds. I don't see either one of them going down easily."

"Do you think this fight ends in a knockout?"

"I won't make that prediction, but the way these two fight, nothing would surprise me. But if I have to make a prediction, this is going to be the best fight of the tournament."

Chip laughed. "That is a good possibility...it will certainly be the most entertaining if yesterday's press conference is any indication." They showed a clip of the press conference, the part at the end when the two boxers started to fight. It got quite the reaction.

After the clip played, Chip Davis responded. "Now that we have you excited about the fight, it looks like we have one of the fighters starting to make his way to the ring." Kenny Allen started walking to the ring first. His walkout music started to blare through the sound speakers at the Aragon Ballroom. He walked out to LL Cool J's, Mama Said Knock You Out." It was an old school rap song, but it got the the point across...perfectly."

Liam was sitting on the dressing table doing some breathing exercises that he was taught so he could stay relaxed. George came around the corner and looked at him. Everything had been discussed from strategy to fighting style. The game plan had been set. There was nothing more to say or anything that George could teach him on how to win this fight. So George simply said. "It's time, kid." Liam looked up with no fear and no confusion on what he had to do tonight. He was about to go to war, but he was at peace, as much as a fighter can be before the first bell. He replied. "Good, let's start the show."

As they walked out of the locker room, Allen's walkout song was finishing up. It finally occurred to Liam that he didn't have any walkout music. He didn't know he could have any. What would be the song that could get him pumped up before a fight, he thought to himself. He said to his trainer. "Why didn't you say we could have walkout music?"

"It wasn't important, but I'm not leaving you high and dry. I have you taken care of."

"Oh, okay...it's not disco because if it is then I'm leaving."

George laughed. "No, I got you something more appropriate. Something worthy of an Irishman." He checked his watch and then looked up to see an usher waiting for his signal. He motioned to the usher that it was time to start. A spotlight shown towards the back of the ballroom onto the stage that appeared to be blocked off and was until now. A bunch of people walked onto the stage along with a couple of bagpipers and Celtic drummers. Liam, walking out from the locker room off to the left of the stage and he looked surprised to see everybody on stage and more than a little confused. George looked at him and said. "Just wait for it. "

Finally the bagpipers started playing the intro to the song. Liam smiled. He recognized the tune. George asked. "You know what this is?"

"Yes, Mo Ghile Mear... It means my gallant hero."

"Yep...I called St. Thomas and they were happy to help with your walkout music. They got the Windy City Drum and Piper crew to play with their Gallic Choir. "

"My grandparents were part of a celtic band. I grew up with this kind of music."

"Looks like they gave you a great music education." Liam thought of them and smiled.

The bagpipe intro lasted for about a minute and then Choir began to sing the song in Gallic. After the singing a short introl, three drummers began to beat what sounded like war drums as the Choir of both men and women continued to sing. It was loud, even more than Allen's walkout song. It certainly got everybody's attention in the Ballroom, which was the point   There were a lot of Irish fans there with Irish National Flags and Chicago city flags. Many of them began to sing and some even waved their flags. You would have thought Ireland was playing in the Six Nations Rugby tournament as excited the Irish fans were. Liam was getting pumped. He wondered if this was how the heroes of 1916 during the revolution. It didn matter, he walked to the ring with his head held high like a warrior poet willing to sacrifice all for the greater good. Kenny Allen shot some dirty looks at the music as if he was trying to say that it didn't bother him and he was going to win anyway.

Chip and Roger commented that they had never seen this before and it may just be the best walkout music in boxing. And that the majority of the crowd was behind Liam after that song. The crowd quieted a little bit after the music ended, but their excitement was electric and radiated throughout the building. The fighters met at the center of the ring, never taking their eyes off one another. There was no fear in both of them, just an intensity that could tear down walls. The ref started talking "Alright, No rabbit punches, no kidney punches, watch the low blows, and in case of a knockdown, you go to the corner I tell you to. Do you understand these rules." Both fighters nodded yes. "Now put your hands up and touch gloves." Kenny Allen said to Liam. "One Round Motherfucker. You're going down in the first round." Liam didn't say anything and just walked back to his corner.

George put Liam's mouth guard in his mouth and said. "Alright, remember, keep your distance and jab. Wait until he throws that two-punch combo and then come underneath both punches and pop him in the ribs like we practiced...keep jabbing...keeping working his ribs. He's going to try and kill you quick with one punch. Remember, It's okay to let him chase you...you set the pace and you'll survive the first round." Liam nodded in agreement. Finally, the first bell rang.

ROUND 10

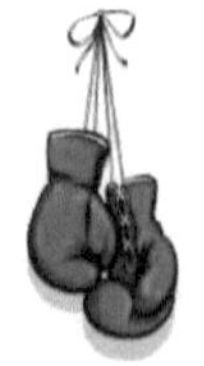

Liam expected the first round to start out slow, both fighters feeling each other out. But Allen came racing out of his corner and immediately started trying to knock him out. Liam moved out the way and kept trying to jab. His three attempts missed as he was trying to keep his distance and stay out of the way of those big hooks. Allen backed him near one of the corners. One of the hooks awkwardly landed on the side of Liam's head. He closed the distance and landed a couple of body shots and then he saw it...the two-punch combo. Just liked he practiced, he moved side to side and came underneath the shots while at the same time putting a couple of hard uppercuts into his opponent's ribs. It was textbook until the third punch came downwards and caught Liam in his right eye. It almost put him on the canvas. He never saw it coming because it was a blind reflex from Allen and he never had enough time to move out of the way.

The punch hurt Liam, it was obvious, but he quickly rolled to his right and was able to escape any more of Allen's punishment. George was surprised too, he never saw it in the film. He yelled to Liam. Keep your distance. And that's how the first round pretty much went. Liam kept jabbing, some landing and some that didn't, but he kept his rhythm...jab, jab...jab, jab. A couple more times, Allen threw his two- punch combo and Liam was able to come underneath and land shots to this ribs. The last time it happened, the second punch caught Liam on the side of the head and made him wince a little bit. It hurt, Liam couldn't deny that. The third punch missed wide, but it didn't matter, the bell rang to end the round. Liam had survived.

He got back to the corner and the cut man immediately started to work on him. There was swelling around his eye and Bill had to put the big coin on him that they kept on ice. Liam was the first to speak. "He hits hard."

George replied. " You knew he wasn't going to take it easy on you."

Liam laughed. "I didn't see that third punch coming down. "

"I didn't either, but here is how you get around it, next time he does it, after you come underneath and move, pivot around backwards and throw your weight into a hook on the opposite...you'll nail him in the eye. You understand." Liam nodded, yes. George continued...I like what you're doing...keep jabbing and working those ribs."

The bell rang for the start of the second round. Allen was mad that he didn't get a knockout in the first and immediately started swinging. Now he was just trying to get a knockout quickly. It was hard for Liam to get out of the way and for the first half of the round he had him mostly on the ropes. Liam just tucked his arms and let Allen swing away, trying to survive the onslaught. He tried jabbing when he could and even pushing off, but Kenny Allen was relentless. People had been saying he was a lot like a young George Foreman and was proving them right. Liam finally was able to push off enough to get off the ropes and create some distance. He jabbed like he was supposed to...jab, jab...jab, jab. After taking some of The Bazooka's punches, he landed a few of his own. Finally it happened...the two-punch combo. He moved underneath it, put one punch into his ribs and pivoted backwards like George said, throwing his weight into a left hook as Allen was coming down with that third punch. Bam! He landed that left hook above Allen's right eye and cut it open.

Chip Davis was the first to say it. "Holy Cow, did you see that. It's the first time Kenny "The Bazooka" Allen has been cut in this tournament. Everybody thought he was invincible and Liam Donnelly just showed he's not."

Roger Bennett replied. "Look at Allen, he stunned...he can't believe he's bleeding."

As they were talking Allen got mad and rushed Liam Donnelly. He pushed him, almost picking him, into a corner and laid a body shot that left Liam winded and then heput a right hook on him that sent Liam to the Canvas. He never saw it coming. Allen, left him alone thinking that he just knocked him out, but Liam jumped and started swinging for his face, but the referee in between the fighters and stopped Liam. It had been scored a knockdown so they had to do the count. It went to four and then the ref let them fight again. Liam rushed Allen, pushing him against the ropes and landed two left hooks cutting Allen again. He punched him as if were in a street brawl. Allen seemed unphased and just started hitting Liam,putting him against the ropes. Everything happened so fast they didn't hear the bell ring, but they both continued to try and hit each other. The ref had to break it up.

Chip Davis replied. "Oh my, lock the door and hide your children because World War 3 just broke out. Folks, the war is here and you're not going to want to miss it."

Roger replied. "If you expected this to end early, don't go to bed just yet, these fighters are not going down easily. Both of them came here to fight and it's going to be bloody."

George got Liam back to his corner. "Don't lose your cool...this is not a street fight."

"I'm not going to let him get away with that."

"Fight smart, but what a hook, I told you it would work. You cut him...he's not invincible...he bleeds just like you. Let him tire himself out when he has you on the ropes, but jab at him with uppercuts like you did before. He's going to run out gas over the next few rounds and then you have him."

They say that every boxing match is won or lost in the middle rounds because it's about who lands the most punches and has the stamina to keep going.   The middle rounds is where your strategy pays off...a few jabs here and there, the perfectly placed uppercut, and timing that right or left hook which will make your opponent back away from you. The feeling out period of the match is over and now you moving and timing your punches just right while waiting to see who makes the first mistake.

That's how it was between Kenny Allen and Liam Kelly. Allen kept getting Liam on the ropes, hoping that his relentless punching would finally put him down. Liam kept going to the body and working his uppercuts to back Allen up and give him the space he needed to jab. His jab was the best thing he had going for him. Both fighters had swelling around the eyes and cuts that their cut men had to work on. Allen became more and more angry that he couldn't knock out Liam. It was a tug of war for the third, fourth, and fifth rounds, but for Liam the strategy was working. When Allen got him on the ropes at the end of the fifth round, he could hear Allen breathing heavy.

It was fairly even by the sixth round, Liam had landed more punches, but it was the sixth where the fight took a turn. Liam was a little slower moving away from that two-punch combo. The right hook grazed him a couple of times. The sixth started out just likes the last three rounds...each fighter taking his time until they found an opening. Liam threw his jab, you could hear it just as crisp as you could in the first round, jab, jab...jab, jab. Finally, Allen got Liam backed into his own corner and just went for it. He threw a hard punch into Liam's left side and it sounded as if a rib might be cracked. Then he threw something that he had never done before...an uppercut. Liam was not prepared for it and it got him right on the nose. That's when his legs went limp. He fell to the canvas trying to hold his nose with his gloves. It hurt like hell. Never once, had he experienced this kind of pain in a fight. Never in one fight had he been hit on the nose or gone down and couldn't pick himself back up. It took him a few seconds to get his bearings and he didn't want to get up, but something inside told him to get up. George was also yelling. "Get up Liam...you can do this...don't quit now...get up!"

Allen was already lifting his hands in the air as if he had just won the fight. Finally, he got his knockout or so he thought. Liam used the ropes and pulled himself up. He yelled at Kenny Allen, who had had his back turned to him, "Hey, ugly...we're not done yet.

Allen turned around and was shocked. This shouldn't have happened, he thought.   It seemed impossible. He slowly walked towards Liam and tried to throw his two punch combo. Liam came underneath both swings, pivoted around backwards, landed a left hook again on Allen' eye. It was starting to bleed faster. Liam found a way to get up and keep going because that's what true fighters do, but he didn't know how long he could keep going. His legs felt like rubber and his left eye was starting to swell shut.

Allen walked towards him and threw wide punch that completely missed Liam. It was easy to get away from it Liam found the strength to hit Allen in the ribs a couple of times and then landed a left hook. Still, Allen wouldn't go down, but it didn't matter, the bell rang to end the sixth round. Liam could hardly walk back to his corner. He had to be helped.

Everybody at Murphy's couldn't take their eyes of the TV's, fearing they would miss that pivotal moment in the fight . Watching the fight was intense Patrons winced every time Liam got hit as if they were feeling the pain too. It was the most exciting event that had happened in the pub since the White Sox won the World Series. This kind of excitement didn't happen very often. One of the regulars sitting at the bar spoke up. "I don't think Liam can last much longer, if he finishes this fight, then it would be a miracle."

Vic gave him a dirty look. "Stop that kind of talk. I think Liam is going to surprise everybody."

Other patrons nodded in agreement. Whether they believed it or not, none of them wanted to jinx Liam by being the asshole who didn't think he could win. Finally the commercials were over and they were intently back watching the fight.

As Liam sat down, Bill took one look at his nose and said. "Your nose is broken. One hit and it's going to start gushing blood and then they'll stop the fight." The nose was already bleeding a little bit and bill stuck Q-tips up his nostrils to stop the bleeding.

Liam said. "I never saw it coming."

George replied. "It happens, but you got up…that's what's important. "

"I can't get this guy down, no matter how much I hit him. I feel like if he hits me one more time then I'm done for."

George looked at him with concern. "Hey, you want me to throw in the towel go home, then that's okay... no shame in it... keep yourself from getting hurt even more."

Liam got angry at the suggestion and yelled out. "Fuck You...we re not stopping this fight."

George smiled. "Good, that's what I want to hear. And you can get this guy down...he's hurt just like you...he's tired just like you."

"What do I do?"

"When the bell rings...you rush him. He'll never expect it. Lower your body like you did in the last fight and just keep pounding on his ribs until you hear something crack. Push him into a corner or on the ropes if you have to. It's t's time to take the fight to him."

The bell rang to start the seventh round. Liam found what was probably his third wind by now. He rushed towards Allen, lowering his body and pushing him towards the ropes. It was so unexpected that Allen didn't know how to defend it, he tried to grab Liam and toss him out of the way, but Liam didn't let him. He fired shot after shot into his opponent's ribs and then out of nowhere came an uppercut that caught Allen right on the nose, causing it to bleed. Liam did what Allen had did to him. Allen was shocked that it happened and he couldn't stand up straight. He fell to his knees, but caught the ropes so he didn't fall all the way.

Chip Davis got excited and yelled. "Kenny Allen goes down... finally, after seven rounds, he goes down."

Roger replied. "If anybody believes that he was still invincible, they don't know. But the ref isn't counting."

"I know, this should be scored a knockdown since his knee touched the canvas. But they're not counting. They're letting Allen get back up. "

"Wow, I've never seen this happen before and look at George Coghlan...he's livid. He's yelling at the ref to start counting, and I don't disagree with him."

"We all know Allen was getting up, but the rules if a knee touches the ground, it's a knockdown. The ref got it wrong and after a 15 second break, he gives the go ahead and let's them start fighting again.

Kenny Allen had never been knocked down before. He was pissed. He chased Liam to try and knock him out, but Liam used the ring and kept his distance. He found his rhythm again with the jab...jab, jab...jab, jab. And then he would through a left hook when

Allen threw a wild punch. Round seven belonged to Liam Kelly. He set the pace. He landed more punches. He wore Kenny Allen down by making him chase him. It was like watching poetry in motion…it was beautiful. Liam didn't completely get out of the round towards the end, he couldn't slip one hook and it nailed him in the eye. He almost went down, but regained his balance by using the ropes. Before Allen could get him again, the bell rang to end the round.

Liam slowly walked back to the corner. His legs felt like rubber. He could barely stand. George and Bill helped him sit down. His left eye was almost shut. The ring doctor walked to check it and to see if he had to stop the fight. Before he could say anything, George responded. "He can see, okay…go check the other guy.

The doctor replied. " Hey, I'm just doing my job."

"Fine, but this is not the time to stop the fight, one round left, let these guys finish it." The Doctor was about to say something, but George got in between him and his fighter and nonchalantly shooed him away. Bill was trying to stop the bleeding in his nose. It was still too close to call whether it would start gushing blood. George held the cold coin to the swelling around his eye. He said.

"Alright... here's the deal since they didn't score the knockdown, on Allen, he probably has you beat on points. If you want to win, you're going to have to knock him out. "

Liam replied. "So go for the knockout."

George smiled. "Yes. You took his leg out from underneath him so they're just tired as yours. And as you probably saw, he's exhausted ...his punches are all over the place. You make him dance with you around the ring. He's going for a knockout too, I guarantee he doesn't care about beating you on points. Make him chase you for about ninety seconds and then you draw him in and let him swing like a wild man."

Liam startedd to understand the strategy. He replied. "Then I take it to the body."

George smiled. "Absolutely...don't let him breath. When he can barely stand, you throw uppercuts and a couple of left hooks."

Liam smiled. "I like it. It's a good plan."

"But you have to wait, you can't do it too early. Now stand up... let's get the blood flowing in those legs. You have three minutes until immortality or failure." Liam nodded as if he understood the seriousness of that statement. George said. "Make it count!" Then he helped Liam stand up and made the fighter slightly jump up and down after taking a drink of water. He wanted to get the blood flowing in his legs.

Allen, who was still sitting down, saw this and was a confused. He didn't know what to make of it. But he stood up because the final round was about to begin. Liam Kelly and Kenny Allen met in the center of the ring and the ref made them touch gloves. Liam didn't say anything. Allen couldn't resist. "Motherfucker...you you're going down... down, motherfucker." Liam just confidently smiled. The ref motioned for them to start the fight.

Chip Davis said. "Here we are in the final round and I don't think anybody believed we'd be here with these two fighters."

Roger replied. "I had a feeling we would get here, but who knows if anybody is still left standing at the end."

"Well these two have gone through a war for only an eight round fight. How are they are still standing, I don't know. But if I had to score it, I have Kenny Allen ahead on the cards because of the two knockdowns against Liam Kelly."

"You may be right, but I think its than most people realize. However, it may take a knockout for Liam Kelly to actually win. "

"You may be right and the final round is about to start between these two brawlers or should I say these two warriors."

Allen didn't come out punching like everybody expected. He was more cautious, waiting to see what Liam would do.

Liam kept his distance and started jabbing...jab, jab...jab, jab. Then he through a left hook and nailed Allen in his bad eye. That's when he started swinging wildly. For Allen, it was a common brawl now. Liam kept out of the way of most of them. A few got through that caught his swolen eye. He could barely see out of it...his vision was pretty much a blur out of that left eye. Ninety seconds went by fast and all of a sudden, he heard George yell out as he slammed the canvas. "Now Liam."

Liam backed towards one of the corners and drew Allen in. He fell for it. He just kept swinging hooks, rights and lefts, not caring about technique. Liam got underneath them and started throwing a flurry of punches to Allen' ribs. Finally, he heard one of them crack. Allen backed away in pain. Liam went after him and took advantage as Allen was holding his side.   He threw two jabs and nailed Allen in the face. Then Allen threw one and hit Liam in the face.   Liam threw two more jabs. Allen threw another landing above Liam's bad eye. They were trading blows as the round was winding down with less than a minute.

A hook from Liam then a right hook from Allen. A jab from Liam then one from Allen. Both fighters weren't stopping until the last bell. Finally, The Bazooka found what strength he had left and threw that two punch combo mixed with the third punch coming down. Liam was so tired that barely missed both of them. The second one grazed his head, but he saw that final punch coming down and remembered despite how tired he was. He pivoted around backwards and put his weight into a left hook and smacked Allen in his swollen eye, but before Allen could react Liam drew the reaming power from his legs and threw a right uppercut nailing Allen in his nose and breaking it again. Kenny "The Bazooka" Allen fell backwards onto the canvas. It was a full knockdown that nobody could deny. The ref backed Liam up to get him away from the fallen Allen.

George could see the time clock from his corner. Thirteen seconds left in the final round. He yelled at the ref. "Starting counting now." Unfortunately, he was moving slow and few seconds went by before he started counting. Allen was hardly moving.

He wasn't trying to get up despite pleas from his corner. The ref counted...10...9...8...7...6...5... still nothing from Allen. He was trying to find the ropes to help pull himself up. The ref continued...4...3...2. But the final bell rang. Allen had saved by the bell.

The crowd went crazy over how exciting the fight had been. However, George was furious. The count had been slow and Liam should have gotten the knockout. Allen wasn't going to get up. He tried to have words with the ref, but he was escorted back to Liam's corner along with his fighter. Allen was helped off the mat and helped back to his corner. The ringside announcer got on the microphone and said. " In a stunning eight round championship fight, we now go to the judges scorecards, please stand by."

It was Liam who was the calm one now and he tried to calm his trainer down in the process. He understood why he was mad, but nothing could be done about it now. What happened...happened." The judges were talking their time. Normally, it took a few minutes to gather everything up and make the announcement. This just made George even more angry. Even Allen's trainer was getting mad and kept trying to walk over and get a sneak peak at the decision. George responded in anger. "This is fucking horseshit." He looked at Liam. "If it takes this long to make a decision, it's probably a controversial one decision and a fighter gets screwed."

Liam looked concerned. "You think that's what's going to happen?"

"I wouldn't be surprised. This should be an easy decision." As they waited, Liam looked down in the crowd and found Molly. He was looking for reassurance. She shrugged her shoulders as if to say she didn't have an answer, but she smiled at him to let him that everything was going to be okay."

George said. "No matter what happens kid, I'm proud of you...you had a hell of a fight. You fought to the end and didn't give up...that's what true fighters do. Win or lose...you've earned the right to be a professional fighter."

Liam smiled. "Thanks...So I'm officially a professional fighter now...no longer a hockey player."

George smiled back. "Yes, you are."

The announcer finally made his way back to the center of the ring. It took nearly ten minutes to get the final scores. All eyes were on the announcer and no one dared look away. He said. "We have the judges score cards. And the scores for this eight round championship fight are...Burt Grogan scores it 84 to 82. Jack Harris scores it 85 to 82. Mario Reyes scores it 84 to 83 to make a unanimous decision. He paused for a moment and then shouted. "And the winner is...Liam "The Crusher " Kelly."

The crowd erupted with excitement. Murphy's Pub celebrated like crazy. Celebratory shots were poured for everybody there. There were some boos from the crowd, predominantly African Americans who were there and felt that Allen got robbed. Liam jumped up and then hugged his trainer. George smiled and patted his fighter on the back. He had not been this excited for a long time, not even when his last champion won a title. Allen was pissed and shook his head in disgust. His trainer even tried playing the race card just to stir up controversy, especially when local press tried to interview Allen. In the midst of his celebration, Liam walked over to Allen and shook his hand. Allen was not happy, but he said as he grabbed Liam's hand. "Congratulations, but I will see you again...this isn't our last fight."

Liam smiled. "Thanks and I don't doubt it."

Molly had climbed into the ring and was waiting for Liam when he came to his corner. She hugged him and said. "Congratulations Liam, that fight was unbelievable."

He smiled "Thank you."

"So I get to sleep with a champion tonight."

He laughed. "So do I."

"Well, Liam Kelly…I think it's safe to say that you're not just another bum from the neighborhood."

Chip Davis came to his corner and interviewed him. It was his first time being interviewed after a boxing match and he didn't really know what to say.

He figured he'd sound like an idiot, but he didn't shy away from it either. Chip asked.

"Congratulations! I think everybody here tonight was shocked that the fight went the full eight rounds considering how easily both of you won your other matches. Are you surprised by the outcome?"

Liam smiled. "I didn't doubt that I could win, but they way the fight went, I guess I am little shocked that it was a unanimous decision."

"I understand that you just retired from being a professional hockey player."

"Yes."

"Do you plan on being a professional fighter and trying to make a career out of it?"

"No, I am… maybe wasn't sure a couple of months ago, but now… the excitement I have felt in the ring, it's got me hooked."

"I read a statistic today that you are the first Irishman to win this Tournament since 1959...what do you think about that?

Liam smiled. "It's a good day for the Irish and I know at least one neighborhood around here that's probably excited so this is really for them."

"What is your goal now?"

Liam smiled. "To be a Champion... I'm sure that's what every fighter says. "

"Do you think you have what it takes to become champion one day?"

George, who was standing next Liam as he was being interviewed, replied before Liam could answer. "I can answer that question better than he can. You know I have trained a lot of champions so I know what I am talking about. This kid has more potential to be the heavyweight champion one day than any fighter I've trained in the last thirty years. The world should take notice because Liam Kelly is a name everybody will know. He's going to be around for a while and his best matched are yet to come."

Chip Davis nodded and replied. "Well, I don't think anybody could argue with that, coming from you."

Liam and his team left the ring and headed to the dressing room. He received a standing ovation from the crowd. It had been one of the greatest boxing matches in Chicago...for some. the best since Tunney knocked out Dempsey at Soldier's Field in 1927 before 104,943 fans.   The fight that became known as, "The Long Count" because when Dempsey knocked Tunney down in the seventh round, the start of the ten count took longer and allowed Tunney to get up when by all accounts he should have been knocked out and Dempsey would have regained the heavyweight championship.

And while the circumstances sounded familiar in comparison to Liam's fight, nobody could deny that both fights had a more distinctive similarity...they turned out to be two of the greatest fights in Chicago and would never be forgotton.   That was the thought that Liam took solace in as he walked back to the dressing room, battered and bruised, before a crowd that was standing and cheering his name."

EPILOGUE

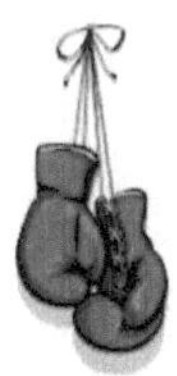

Liam was greeted with a hero's welcome when he arrived Murphy's Pub. It was an impromptu after party and after getting fixed up by doctors, Liam could think of no better place to celebrate his victory. While not one for parties anymore, even George was happy to be, there… after all, he stilled liked a good Guinness every once in a while. Whiskey flowed like an endless waterfall. And pints of Guinness were passed around until the kegs were empty. It was a better than St. Patrick's Day.

Vic quieted everybody down and proposed a toast. "To Liam Kelly…the All Chicago Heavyweight Boxing Champion and making this neighborhood proud again."

Liam smiled and replied as he pointed to Molly. "Raise a Glass to her too…she won the Women's Division."

Vic raised his glass again. "To the prettiest champion in Chicago. Liam probably couldn't do better." The crown in the pub cheered. Molly couldn't help but laugh. As people were celebrating and Liam was shaking hands, George pulled him aside. "I have some good news for you." He introduced Liam to Pricilla. "This is Pricilla Hogan…she is a boxing promoter…took over the business when her husband died. Any she got you a fight if you're interested. "

"With who," Liam asked."

Pricilla replied. "Davis Dean, he's ranked 15th in the world and we need to replace the guy who he was supposed to fight. It's in six weeks and it's the main event. It's yours if you want it."

"Hell yeah…do you think I'm ready?"

George winced. "We will have to get you healed up fast, but yes, with good training, I think you can be ready."

"My first professional fight, fuck yeah!"

"Well, I'm glad that you're excited, but now the real work begins. And the road to being a champion isn't called easy street…it's going to be hard. Tonight won't be the worst beating you take. Starting on Monday we get to see what you're really made of because the toughest opponent we all face is the little voice inside that says that's not good enough…and that's when we know the real work begins. Are you sure, you still want to do this?"

Liam smiled because he knew what George was trying to do..he was trying to motivate him… to see if he had the heart to be a champion. "I'm not going anywhere and I will be definitely be there on Monday. Bright and early."

"That's what I want to hear. Now the other piece of news I have is I made a bet for you. The odds against you were 8 to 1 so I put six grand on you. You won forty-eight thousand dollars to help get you started with training expenses and with the thirty thousand you got from the tournament, you shouldn't have to work anymore…you can train full time."

Liam was shocked. "Holy shit…no kidding. Where did you get six grand."

"Don't worry about me, I got plenty of money…lot more than you."

Liam laughed. "Oh yeah"

"And just to help you out, you won't have to pay me until you really start making some big paydays. I just wanted you to not have to work a job and be a professional at the same time. Your journey is going to be tough enough. Now go celebrate because come Monday, the fun is over." Liam smiled and walked off to get another beer. Pricilla gave George a surprised look. "You bet on your fighter and won him some money, you're not taking a salary for the first year...is it safe to say you're officially not retired!"

George replied. "I guess I never was."

"Well, if this is your last hurrah as a trainer then I have a feeling you picked a good one."

"I agree, but he hasn't truly been tested yet, we still have a long way to go and I've been fooled by great fighters before."

Liam and Molly laid in bed. She did most of the work when it came to making love since he was still battered from the fight, but it still felt fantastic for the both of them. Their Championship belts sat next to each at the foot of the bed. Liam and Molly smiled as they gazed upon the belts, both equally proud of what they other had done. They had pretty much spent every night together the past week since they had first got together and not once had talked about it. Both of them were of the same mind just to let things naturally happen, but the girl inside Molly needed more.   She had to know what this really was and could tell that Liam was not the type of guy to open up and share his feelings She said. I hate to be that type of girl, but I am curious, what is this between us?"

"You mean, are we boyfriend and girlfriend?"

"Something like that...I'm not saying that we have to define this, but I guess, I want to know that we are more than just two fighters hooking up."

"What's wrong with that?"

Molly gave him a dirty look. "If that's all you're looking for, fine, I just want to know. Not saying this would end, but just want to know what you're thinking."

"I usually don't spend a week hooking up with someone...If I spend this much time with you then it means that I like you, maybe not enough to get married, but definitely want to keep seeing you."

She smiled. "Good, because I want to see you again. And, not I'm not expecting a marriage proposal."

"I can't promise you that you will ever get one from me. I don't know if a fighter's life and marriage can work, especially if you throw kids into the mix."

She laughed. "Now, we are talking about kids…that's a little fast, don't you think?"

" Ha! I'm just saying kids may be in the cards, but those things may not work with a fighter's life and right now, I'm going to focus on my new career. It doesn't mean we can't be together."

"I know, just giving you a hard time and you're right, it doesn't mean we can't still see each other."

Liam smiled. "Good…" Liam was cut off because of a knock at the door. It was a little past one a.m. so it seemed strange. It was late. He put on a pair of gym shorts and answered the door. There were three men standing there that he didn't recognize, but they looked like men he shouldn't be messing with."

The man in the middle responded. "Hey Liam or should I say…Champ!"

Liam replied. "Hi, what can I do for you?"

"It's about your father and his bad luck."

Liam gave him a strange look. "I don't have anything to do with my father…whatever problems he has with you...you deal with him. I have nothing to do with it. "

"Unfortunately, it doesn't work that way." Before Liam could say anything, one of the men pulled a gun and they bullied their way into the apartment. Liam shouted. "What the fuck man" Instinct took over and he punched the other guy who didn't have a gun. Then he went for the man who had been talking. The man with the gun, pointed it at Liam and then the man who had done the talking replied in anger. "Cool it Champ! We're just here to talk...don't get yourself hurt."

Molly had come out of the bedroom with only a sheet wrapped around the body. She gasped when she the three men. The main guy responded to her. "Well hello. Just stand there quietly and be cool." Then he turned to Liam, "Now, as I was saying, this is about your father and now it concerns you too. My name is Mr. Abbot and I represent a man that your father owes a lot money too."

Liam shot him an angry look. "Again, not my problem...he can deal with his own shit."

"I wish that were the case, but my employer has a strict policy that when he's owed money...he get's his money no matter what. So when someone can't pay...their family pays the debt."

"I don't have anything to do with man...he walked out on me and my mother ten years ago."

"But you're still related to him. And that makes it your problem too."

"The fuck it does, I don't care what you do to him to settle the debt...you can kill him for all I care."

Mr. Abbot smiled. "Doesn't matter. Even if he ends up dead, then it becomes your debt and I don't think you want to end up that way, especially with such a promising boxing career."

"Let me get this straight. If he doesn't pay you then you come after me. "

"That's the way it works?"

"Why?"

"Because to be a successful businessman like my employer, you always get what's owed to you and at the end of the day, someone always ends up paying cause its better than the alternative."

"How much does he owe?"

"Forty-five Grand... he asked for extra points if he didn't have to pay up front...tripled the debt. And the vig started running tonight. It's twenty percent a week. You know what a vig is, don't you."

Liam gave him a dirty look. "Yes, of course I do, but I don't have that kind of cash."

Mr. Abbot laughed. "You just won thirty grand tonight…you're two- thirds away from settling the debt."

"Fuck you…that's for my training expenses."

"Pop Quiz…how much training can you do when you're dead!"

Liam didn't say anything for a moment. "What do you want from me?"

"Simple…take care of your father's debt and nothing happens."

"And if I don't… your friend with the gun pays me a visit."

"See, you're smart for a boxer. But just in case you don't think we're serious…"The other two men grabbed Liam and moved him towards the kitchen counter despite him struggling, wearing only his boxers. They put his left hand on the counter. He struggled to get free, but both men put together, were stronger and pinned him down. Then the main guys took the butt of the gun and slammed it on three of Liam's fingers. Liam screamed in pain. The fingers were easily broken and bent out of shape. Liam in a screaming fit, yelled. "Fuck you, you fucking cock sucker." It wasn't eloquent, but he made his point with the insult.

Mr. Abbot laughed. "Say whatever you want, but the debt is now yours too. It may be harder to fight with broken fingers, but you can still fight. The next time, you won't be so lucky. Remember that if you decide not to pay or try to fight back." He pulled out a business card and dropped it on the counter. "When you're ready to pay, call the number on the card and we will tell you what to do next." The three men walked out of the apartment, but before they were completely gone. Mr. Abbot said. "Have a nice night...Champ!"

There's an ugly side to boxing, far beyond glory or defeat in the ring. Liam had learned a lot about the sport, but he had been shielded from the dark side until now. And no one could really teach you about the dark side...they were lessons you had to learn on your own. You learn through experience and no one can do that for you. Such was the law of life when it came to boxing. For not all battles are fought inside the ring...a lesson that Liam "the Crusher" Kelly started to learn. George had said from day one that the road to being a champion wouldn't be easy. It was brutal and always a constant battle. Liam, well, he just realized, that was a fucking understatement!

The story of Liam *"The Crusher"* Kelly
will continue in book 2...